Richard Lynott O'Malley

Wyoming and Indian Melodies and Other Poems

Richard Lynott O'Malley

Wyoming and Indian Melodies and Other Poems

ISBN/EAN: 9783744708142

Printed in Europe, USA, Canada, Australia, Japan

Cover: Foto ©Andreas Hilbeck / pixelio.de

More available books at **www.hansebooks.com**

WYOMING

AND

INDIAN MELODIES

AND OTHER POEMS

BY

RICHARD LYNOTT O'MALLEY

———

PHILADELPHIA:

KETTERLINUS PRINTING HOUSE, Arch and Fourth Streets.

1891.

PREFACE.

The question may be asked—and very properly, too—why the author has been induced to submit for publication many of the poems contained in this volume. The answer is this: Not that the compositions just alluded to are of marked literary excellence, nor that they possess any singularly valuable historic merit, but simply because, owing to the topical characteristic of the subject-matter involved, their embodiment in this work was strenuously requested by friends in Wyoming Valley. This, however, is not said with a view to escape censure; far from it. Such a measure were, indeed, worse than idle ; for harsh criticism follows everything new just as inevitably as night follows the day. The purpose of the statement is to disarm the critic, if possible, of any preconceived notion he may entertain as to a definite degree of excellency to which every work of art must necessarily attain, irrespective of its subject-matter, its character, its motive, or the principle inculcated.

Sufficient fairness may be frequently rendered by criticizing objectively rather than subjectively. Inferences should be drawn from what is actually in the book, not from what ought to be in it; not from a creation of something entirely new, having shape merely in the mind of the reader.

R. L. O.

FAREWELL TO WYOMING, ... 7
BY FAIR SUSQUEHANNA, ... 8
DISAPPOINTMENT. LIFE, ... 9
THE GOOD MAN, ... 10
LORD BYRON, ... 10
A SUSQUEHANNA LEGEND, ... 11
CAROL TO WYOMING, ... 12
THE OLD SCHOOL BELL, ... 13
FRUITION, ... 14
GLYCÆA, ... 15, 95
RECOLLECTIONS OF CHILDHOOD, ... 16
LOVE BY THE SEA, ... 16
TO MY FRIEND F. M. TO MR. LINK, ... 17
LINES FOR A SCHOOL-GIRL'S AUTOGRAPH ALBUM, ... 17
TO WYOMING, ... 18
THE FINAL LEAF, ... 18–20
TO FRANK MARTIN, ... 20
NESHANNOCK LEGEND, ... 20–22
TO CLEMATIS, ... 22, 52, 53, 96
THE SONG OF THE OLD SCHOOL-BELL, ... 23
THE LOVER'S LAMENT, ... 24
LOVE AND FANCY, ... 25
FRIENDSHIP'S TONE AND LAUGH, ... 26
CAMPBELL'S LEAP, ... 27–31
ADIEU, TILL WE MEET AGAIN, ... 31
O SWEET THE DREAM OF BY-GONE DAYS, ... 32
SONG OF PARTING COMPANIONS, ... 33
MIDNIGHT VISIONS 33
TO ANNA, ... 34
ANNA, ... 35
THEY SAY THAT THE FAIRIES HAVE POWER, ... 36
FRIENDSHIP'S CHAIN, ... 37
TO CLEMATIS, ON HIS THIRTEENTH BIRTHDAY, . . 38
SONG TO THE BUTTERCUP, ... 38
O WHERE IS THE BLOOM THAT BLUSHED, ... 39
SONNET TO THE OLD YEAR. SONNET TO F. B, ... 40
SONG OF CUPID, ... 41
GULA AND LILY AND NET, ... 41

6   *CONTENTS.*

FATHER OF THE NIGHT AND MORN. MINEPHTHAH,   . 42
QUARREL OF BRUTUS AND CASSIUS, ... 43–45
THE CHIEFTAIN AND HIS BARD, ... 46–48
"BREAK, BREAK, BREAK!" 48
THE GRIEF OF AVOCA, ... 49
SPRING SMILES AGAIN, ... 50–52
CHRISTMAS BELL, ... 54
IS HE DEAD? 55
ALKRANE'S SONG, ... 56–58
AUTUMN IN PREHISTORIC WYOMING. 58
SCENE IN PREHISTORIC WYOMING, ... 59
A LACKAWANNA LEGEND, ... 60
TALAKEENA'S CHASE, ... 61–63
ALKRANE'S SONG OF LOVE, ... 63–65
ALKRANE'S PROPHECY, ... 65–69
ALKRANE'S SONG, MAUKANAW, ... 69
CONFLICT BETWEEN TALAKEENA AND MAUKANAW, ... 70–74
TALAKEENA'S BISON CHASE, ... 74
TALAKEENA AT EVENING, ... 75
TALAKEENA'S BATTLE WITH THE WHITE MEN, ... 76–80
NONSENSE AND NOISE, ... 80
WEEP NOT. THE PIG AND THE DRUNKARD, ... 81
RECOLLECTIONS OF SCHOOL DAYS, ... 82–87
MY SOUL, ... 87
TO MY SISTER MARY, ON HER FOURTEENTH BIRTHDAY, . . . 87–90
ENTOMBED COAL MINERS AT SOUTH WILKESBARRE, ... 90
EVENING IN SUMMER, ... 91
CALEPSYCHE, ... 92
GOOD-BYE, MY FRIEND. LINES FOR AN AUTOGRAPH ALBUM, . . 93
TO MISS M., ... 94
AN ANSWER. PHOEBE, ... 95
TO CALLIE, ... 96
ON THE BANKS OF SUSQUEHANNA. TRUE HAPPINESS, ... 97
MY REPENTANCE, ... 98
I'M GROWING OLD, ... 98
EPISTLE TO F. M., ... 99–102
AN EARNEST THANKSGIVING; OR THE DRUNKARD AND HIS BOY, 102–105
A PRAYING AND TRUSTING, ... 105
MORNING HYMN, ... 105
EVENING HYMN, ... 105
OUR DUTY, ... 106
THE HAUNTED FOREST, ... 106–111
PROMETHEUS BOUND. A MONODY, . . . 112–120

WYOMING AND INDIAN MELODIES

AND OTHER POEMS.

WYOMING.

O sweet is the vale of Wyoming and mild !
It gave my first light, on my childhood it smiled,
And it will smile on my manhood, for how could I part
With a friend that's implanted so deep in my heart !
O had I the tongue of a honey-voiced bird,
Then, then would thy praise, fair Wyoming, be heard ;
Aye, then I might tell, with a spell-giving sound,
The magic which dwells on thy bosom around.

But I weep as I gaze on thy beauteous scene—
On thy hills and thy forests in slumber serene,
On thy river which forth in its majesty sweeps—
O I weep, and my spirit within me weeps,
For I know that a mortal could never reveal
Half the magic I see, half the rapture I feel ;
But a wish I can give, though my best praises fail :
May thy bloom never fade, sweet Wyoming, my vale !

FAREWELL TO WYOMING.

Wyoming, sweet valley, I leave thee in pain !
  For with thee were my happiest hours ;
Alas ! I with my playmates may never again
  Be blessed with the charm of thy bowers !

O wild are thy mountains and forests, so rare,
　　And rugged and steep are thy hills,
And sweet is the sound of thy rivulets fair,
　　And rushing, meandering rills.

Wide-spread through thy woodland and over thy plains
　　Bloom flowers, unrivaled in hues,
By soft zephyrs kissed, and cooled by the rains,
　　And nurtured by evening dews.

Thy scenery, thy wildness, thy beauty, thy blush,
　　When smiled on by fairest of skies,
O how could I paint without dipping my brush
　　In paints of the rainbow dyes !

Is it thus, I wonder, with every heart?
　　Does each think his land is the best?
Does each gladden to meet, does each sadden to part
　　With the scene which in childhood has blest?

Ah, deep is my sadness !　I leave thee to-day—
　　Big and warm was the tear which now fell :
Yes, my Eden, I sigh—for, I can not well say,
　　" Wyoming, sweet valley, farewell ! "

BY FAIR SUSQUEHANNA.

By fair Susquehanna my childhood has been :
　　There I romped when a wild wanton boy ;
And 'tis there that my playmates and I could be seen
　　When our bosoms heaved lightest with joy.

There hailed we the storm, hailed the sunlight which stole
　　To the bower and nook where we met—
Ay, a spark of its ardor still glows in my soul,
　　And it warms me to happiness yet !

Dame nature, my river, still smiles upon thee
　　As she smiled in my infancy's day ;
Yet I sigh, though thy voice and thy laugh welcome me,
　　For my playmates ; O stream, where are they ?

Enough that I view thee alone and downcast,
  Where together so oft we have played ;
Enough that I sigh for dear friends of the past
  Who with me this same landscape surveyed !
Yes, aged am I, and the last of my race,
  And the world is estranged from me ;
Yet, though my old playmates I ne'er shall embrace,
  I may live, Susquehanna, for thee.

DISAPPOINTMENT.

I awoke at the dawn of a school holiday,
  And the heavens with clouds were o'ercast ;
And I prayed for the sunlight's tiniest ray,
  But the rain fell heavy and fast.

Then I calmed my heart with the hope that soon
  It would clear ; and the sun at last
I saw, and I hoped, but alas ! at noon
  The rain fell heavy and fast.

Now faster and faster poured the rain,
  Still I hoped through the storm and the blast ;
And the night came frowning ; my hopes were vain,
  For the rain fell heavy and fast.

Ah ! my holiday fled on her own rainy wind,
  And my hopes followed close on her flight ;
But the cold disappointment still clouded my mind
  Which had chilled me from morning till night.

Then I thought " It is thus with full many a life ;
  Each hope comes and goes like a breath ;
And the mortal toils on with vain hope through the strife,
  From childhood to manhood and death."

LIFE.

Life is a rose bush ; we hail fortune's blush,
Nor think of the ills that have tricked us ;
Thus, pleased by the roses we've plucked from the bush,
We forget the thorns that have pricked us.

THE GOOD MAN.

I met a man on Life's thronged way,
  And thought at once that man was good :
I learned to know him ; strange to say,
  Still thought I that the man was good.
     A virtue loves he, not for praise,
     But for that virtue's sake ; to daze
     By show disdained he.   Years his ways
I watched, and still, O still I thought him good.

     Ah ! ask you why, amidst the van
     Of heroes, place I him who ran
     His race of life in goodness true ?
     Ask you what marvel did he do ?
     Duty to God, and self, and man !
     He ended good as he began ;
       Such men, alas, are few !

LORD BYRON.

Lord Byron was a gifted man,
  A poet and a chief ;
His conscience, like a tattered book,
  Could never get *re-leaf*.

Strong was his mind and strong his frame,
  But crooked was his *sole ;*
His lips of beauty seemed a-part,
  And yet they formed a (w)*hole*.

His heart, though like a *dandy-lion*,
  Possessed a wondrous power ;
It bloomed and flourished like a plant
  That you would *call-a-flower*.

He helped the Greeks in freedom's cause,
  With fortune, fire and sword ;
Nor lowered his colors in the fight
  Till he became *deep-lowered*.

Ah, there he died, great lord, in Greece,
  Beneath a Turkey's feet,
In *a-dry-attic* suite of rooms,
  Unlike to Heaven sweet.

A SUSQUEHANNA LEGEND.

'Twas moonlight on fair Susquehanna's wave,
And the rays a sad sheen to the ripples gave ;
Still the ripples smiled, and the ripples hummed,
As if to all gloomness and sadness benumbed.
And every soft breeze from the western shore
  Was laden with sighs from a maiden fair,
Who watched 'neath the willows which shadowed her o'er,
  And she sighed and she wept as she watched alone there.
Ah ! deep sighed the maiden, and tears filled her eyes,
And the willows wept too and re-echoed her sighs.

Now far o'er the water toward Pittston she glanced,
And now on the ripples which prattled and danced ;
Still the ripples smiled, and the ripples hummed,
As if to all yearning and sadness benumbed.
" Ah, love ! " she sighed, " Why, why this delay ?
  Hast thou broken the vow in thy bosom deep hid ?
No, my loved one—no, no ! naught else keeps thee away
  Than death—than death, and such Heaven forbid ! "
Then deep sighed the maiden, while tears filled her eyes,
And the willows wept too and re-echoed her sighs.

Far over the waters she gazed in vain ;
Then gazed on the ripples, and back again ;
Still the ripples smiled, and the ripples hummed,
As if to all yearning and sadness benumbed.
Lo, now the sound of an oar she hears :
  Sweet, sweet is her transport, her sighs are no more ;
Alas ! soon flee her smiles as the vessel nears ;
  She sees a white form at the plashing oar.
Then deep sighed the maiden, while tears filled her eyes ;
And the willows wept too and re-echoed her sighs.

She stared at the vessel as one insane,
Then stared at the ripples, then back again ;
Still the ripples smiled and the ripples hummed,
As if to all sorrow and sadness benumbed.
Lo, the figure in white from her bosom distressed
   Moaned aloud, " O, my brother—my brother is dead !
He sent me to bear his last wish to thy breast,
   The wish to embrace thee where angels are wed ! "
Then deep sighed the maiden, while tears filled her eyes ;
And the willows wept too and re-echoed her sighs.

Then shrieked she, " Alas ! left alone to deplore,"
Then plunged neath the ripples, to rise nevermore ;
Still the ripples smiled, and the ripples hummed,
As if to all woe and all sorrow benumbed.
And now, at each twilight, there oft may be seen,
   When 'tis moonlight on fair Susquehanna's wave,
A maiden white robed on the willowy green,
   As she weeps and sighs o'er a watery grave.
Ah, still sighs the maiden, while tears fill her eyes ;
And the willows weep too and re-echo her sighs.

CAROL TO WYOMING.

Forgive me, Wyoming, this boldness
   Of pouring my rapture to thee ;
But how can I slumber in coldness
   When thou art a warm friend to me !

I know that my tongue ill portrays thee,
   But, when thy sweet smiles on me burn,
O, how can I help but to praise thee,
   And give thee one smile in return !

Ah, forget I the gifts thou hast given,
   Which bless my fond playmates' and me ?
O, the sun shall forget to climb heaven,
   Ere I am forgetful of thee !

Thou hast given the glad river I row in,
 And thy hills are my playmates' and mine :
Thou hast given the wild forest I go in
 For bird-nest and fruit tree and vine.

It is thou that has given the fierce mountains,
 And the peak where bold Campbell met death ;
And 'tis thou that hast given cool fountains,
 Whose waters leap fathoms beneath.

How I thrill as I mingle my laughter
 With the spray as it laughs on the rocks !
While its lightnings and thunders peal after
 And the crows flutter round me in flocks !

O, thou wilt forgive me, Wyoming,
 This rapture in wildness to thee,
For 'twas thou that first ledst me a-roaming,
 And taughtst this wild freedom to me.

Then here's to thee, sweetest of valleys !
 From thy own mountain spray do I quaff ;
May thy zephyr which round me now dallies
 Ever echo thy praise in my laugh.

THE OLD SCHOOL-BELL.

I pause upon Life's worn threshold,
 And gaze with a weary eye
Far backward through memory's vista,
 Where many quaint relics lie.
I see the old school-bell swinging,
 Imparting familiar chimes,
And it brings unto me a vision
 Of far away by-gone times.
The tones have the same wild clearness,
 The very same tale they tell ;
O, that mortal could live ever onward
 Unchanged like the old school-bell.

Still the same does that school-bell clamor,
　　But not to my ears, alas !
Nor the ears of my dear old playmates ;
　　It speaks to a different class.
It calls them and laughs as it calls them,
　　And sets them afresh at their toil ;
And tells them that perseverance
　　Uncovers the richest spoil.
Ring on, ring on, O my school-bell ;
　　Let other breasts heave to thy swell ;
Let other hearts learn how to love thee,
　　Be ever the old school-bell.

Of all my old class, my companions,
　　None, none now remains but me ;
And I, too, am fast approaching
　　That boundless eternity.
Thus, one after one we are withered :
　　The bell never sees our woe,
But onward to other school boys
　　She laughs in her course to and fro.
Her tones have the same wild clearness,
　　The very same tale they tell ;
O, that mortal could live ever onward,
　　Unchanged like the old school-bell.

FRUITION.

Fruition, phantom of delight,
Thou sweet, beguiling, joyous sprite,
Come, free my heart from worldly care,
And re-instate youth's pleasures there ;
And like a blessing from above,
Teach my dull spirit how to love ;
And teach it, teach it to forget
The long-lived sadness it has met.
Thou fairy bird of fleeting wings,
The potent charms thy magic brings

Assuage, expel my keenest pain,
And smile my soul to joy again ;
Around my weary head then hover,
And, with the rapture of a lover,
Impart, with all thy energy,
Thy fondest, sweetest melody.

O now thou seemest near to me,
So near I fear of losing thee,
And whispers vague torment my brain,
Hinting that all my hope is vain.
O, that our arms might interlace,
And lock for aye in sweet embrace !
Then, what were worldly care to me,
For life itself were ectasy !

GLYCEA.

They tell me a tale of the early world,
How angels from Heaven's own portals were hurled,
Who, awhile, had forgot their celestial birth,
And forgot their high bliss for the maidens of earth.
For a time, my Glycæa, I could not believe
That Heaven was risked for the daughters of Eve ;
I could not believe, till—O, how shall I say !
Till I saw—till I saw thy charms brighten the day ;
Then I knew why the angels forgot their high bliss,
For who would not err for a transport like this ?

Again have I heard of a mystic parterre,
Where lovers in dalliance fond ever were,
While their eyes, like the starlight, that Eden illumed,
And their kisses and smiles into rosebuds bloomed.
O, had I a garden, in whose magic bowers
All my prayers, all my wishes might bud into flowers,
Whose odors might murmur my love-sighs for me,
What a wreath should I twine, O, Glycæa, for thee !
What a wreath fed with love, O, 'twould never decay !
But fed with such true love, 'twould blossom for aye.

RECOLLECTIONS OF CHILDHOOD.

O ! fond recollections of innocent childhood,
    Again do ye speak of my long-faded joy:
Ye lead me once more to my dearly-loved wildwood,
    Where I with my brothers have played when a boy.
Again do I stray 'mid the shadowy bowers,
Hard by the green meadow bespangled with flowers—
O, 'twas here that my heart knew its happiest hours,
    In pleasures which nothing I thought could destroy.

Still the same do the songsters pour gladsome their number,
    It seems that they know me, and wish to rejoice ;
But where are the voices whose echoes now slumber,
    And where are the hearts which throbbed here to my
        voice ?
Go, ask I the lark in yon sweet-scented clover ;
Ask the bee and the butterfly there as they hover :
They will say that the days of my brothers are over,
    And the graves in that meadow they took for their
        choice.

O ! pictures of childhood, so bright and enchanting,
    How fairy-like now in the present ye seem ;
For years ye have haunted, and still ye are haunting,
    My soul in each idle and wandering dream.
Fare-thee-well, O thou scene of my earliest pleasure !
Yes, thee, whom I claim as my mind's dearest treasure !
To me thou may'st give empty joy without measure,
    But ne'er can'st restore my lost rapturous stream !

LOVE BY THE SEA.

O ! lovely the form of the maiden,
    As she wandered alone by the sea,
And lovely with beauty enladen
    Were the eyes which fell fond upon me :
And I met that gaze in a trance-like daze,
    And I lingered awhile by the sea.

Sweet, sweet were the moments that followed,
  As together we strayed by the sea,
And sweet were the whispers, and hallowed
  The vow which gave heaven to me ;
And we sealed our bliss with a votive kiss
  As we lingered awhile by the sea.

Now blissful each calm twilight minute,
  The fleet minute we spend by the sea ;
We smile, and each wavelet has in it
  A smile for my loved one and me ;
And the starlight streams, and our lovelight beams,
  As we linger in bliss by the sea.

TO MY FRIEND F. M.,
NICK-NAMED "FRA DIAVOLO" (THE DEVIL'S BROTHER.)

O, Fra Diavolo, well have they named you !
  A fitter name is it than any other,
Except the name which by right should have claimed you,
  And that's the aforesaid gentleman's brother.

LINES FOR A SCHOOL-GIRL'S AUTOGRAPH ALBUM.

Dear girl, this book I can not brook !
What ! write you something comic?
Nay, writing much of that, and such,
Doth give a man the thumb-ache :
'Tis worse than all that school-girl's scrawl,
Which overturns the stomache.

TO MR. LINK.

When Link was masked in dress, I wis,
He seemed a real linking miss ;
But since he's got his pants, we think,
He seems a real *missing link*.

TO WYOMING.

O, many a rustic bard has sung
  Thy praises, fair Wyoming vale !
But the sweet accents of each tongue
  Scarce flew beyond his native dale,
And when his last breath died away,
His songs all perished with his clay.

So fares each bard ; e'en as a flower
  Whose death fast follows on its bloom ;
He breathes a sweetness to his bower,
  Then with that sweetness fades in gloom :
And though Wyoming be his theme,
Even thou, Wyoming, still dost dream.

Yet now and then thy slumber breaks,
  When stranger bards bid thee rejoice :
In Campbell's Gertrude wild awakes
  Thy loveliness to Fancy's voice ;
And Halleck, too, has breathed thy name,
And sung thy praise in words of flame.

O, that some minstrel son of thine
  Could wake thy children from their sleep,
And tell them how thy glories shine,
  That they might praise or, failing, weep !
Then blest were I, though my faint songs
Should perish 'mid the rapturous throngs.

THE FINAL LEAF.

ON DR. HOLMES' "LAST LEAF."

He wandered far and near :
For many a long year
    He was gone ;
But now he has returned,
With wrinkled face all burned
    By the sun.

His cane is in his hand—
Poor man, he could not stand
    But for that !
It aids his feeble bones
As his footsteps knock the stones
    Pit-a-pat.

Now everybody says
That in his younger days,
    Long ago,
Each pretty smiling lass
Would whisper as he'd pass,
    "That's my beau ! "

But now he slowly walks,
And scarcely ever talks,
    He's so worn :
While at his yellow pants
He casts a vacant glance,
    So forlorn.

For those he loved so dear
He grieves with sigh and tear
    And a moan.
Upon each mouldering mound,
On top, and all around,
    Moss is grown.

The lonely willows sigh
As walks he thoughtful by
    Each little hill :
They sigh, and gently weep
Above his friends that sleep
    There so still.

I've often heard it told
That this man, now so old,
    When quite young,
Was blest with beauties great,
With well-shaped face and pate,
    And loose tongue.

But now, his features grim,
Make a scarecrow out of him,
    Tall and spare,
With crooked nose, and back
As if a peddler's pack
    Rested there.

I know it is quite wrong
For me to stand so long
    Eyeing him ;
But that old coat of blue,
And hat with corners, too,
    Look so prim.

And if I should live in grief,
To be a Final Leaf
    In the fall,
Let people wink and scoff,
And laugh as I now laugh ;
    I've earned it all.

TO FRANK MARTIN.

As I was at the gate one day,
    And just about to start-in,—
Pardon me, decent folks, I pray,
    But, oh ! I met Frank Martin !

NESHANNOCK LEGEND.

(The Neshannock is a small stream which runs through Newcastle city, in Western Pennsylvania.)

O, few were the dwellings where Newcastle stands,
And few were the tillers that break the wide lands,
But Neshannock sped on, as it speeds on to-day,
Now sighing and sad, now heedless and gay.

It sighs for the deed which discolored its sands,
Where now by the Mill street bridge it is spanned ;
And 'tis heedless and gay when afar from the site,
Where that Mill street horror affrighted the night.

'Twas midnight in June, and the moon shone as mild
  As ever she shone in her mildness before,
When a maiden appeared, O, 'twas Eve's fairest child !
  So lovely she seemed on Neshannock's calm shore.

She smiled to the wavelets, that smile they returned ;
  She sighed to the zephyr, it gave back a sigh ;
She glanced at the starlight, and brighter it burned,
  And blent with the lovelight which blazed in her eye.

Why looks she so oft at the hillock beyond,
  Where towers that mansion, all dark and alone ?
Her parents are there, unsuspecting and fond ;
  They slumber, nor dream that their dear one has flown.

She has flown, she has flown, and a minute or two
  May place her loved plow-boy for aye at her side ;
Then adieu to her parents, a lasting adieu,
  For her path is to be on the billowy tide.

A footstep now starts her, she turns her fair head ;
  In a moment her welcoming smile flits away ;
The sound has deceived her, for strange is the tread,
  And that cloak and that hat but renew her dismay.

The stranger draws near, and, with low, muffled voice,
  Says, "My sweet one, choose me, for thy lover now
      dreams."
"Back, back !" shouted she ; "rather death for a choice!"
  See, his cloak moves aside, and a dagger there gleams !

"Come, swear thou art mine !" he commands, as he clasps
  Her arm in a gentle, yet menacing air.
Like a flash, from his girdle the dagger she grasps,
  And pierces his breast. Lo, he falls in despair !

"Ah, my loved one !" he moans, "how accursed was the
      jest !"
  She shrieked, while her brain with new frenzy was fired,
"'Tis my lover ! O God !" Then she fell on his breast,
  And sighed with her slain, and, both sighing, expired.

Fair Neshannock sighed too, and still does she prate
　In sighs as she kisses the spot where they died ;
But their friends never learned how they met their sad fate,
　For they knew not the language the prating stream
　　　sighed.

　　And up to this day the intent passer-by
　　May hear in Neshannock's low murmuring sigh
　　The tale that I've told, with the sad melody,
　　Just as Neshannock rehearsed it to me.

TO CLEMATIS.

　'Tis bliss to me, Clematis, dear,
　Yea, double bliss, that thou art near ;
　That thou art near, and feel'st the thrill
　Of all my love.　More blissful still
　Am I that thy fond heart returns
　The flame with which my bosom burns ;
　For rare it is to meet a soul
　Which gives back all the love it stole ;
　And rare it is to find a breast
　Which makes a loving bosom blest ;
　And rare, O rare it is to find
　Two loves that have, like ours, entwined.
　Then doubly blest am I by thee ;
　I cling to thee, and thou to me.
　Happy the hearts that link their powers
　In such a flawless chain as ours.

　How sweet ! how sweet !　But O, my friend,
　Can this last ? will it never end ?
　Ah ! I have often loved before
　With such a love as I love thee ;
　But soon, too soon away was tore
　The heart which was such bliss to me.
　Some were called off by God's own grace.
　And some, alas, were false !　O base,

O base the wretch that plays the part
Of trifling with another's heart !
But O, Clematis, true as steel,
The source of all my present weal,
Think not, think not, I deem thee so !
No, no ! Let such thoughts hell-ward go !
Enough, that thou art true to me ;
Enough, that I'm so blessed to be
With all my soul a friend to thee.

THE SONG OF THE OLD SCHOOL-BELL.

'Mid memory's fondest voices
  That sound in my revery,
There is one that has cheered my boyhood,
  And whose echoes still live in me.
'Tis the voice of the bell that boldly
  Swung over the school-house door,
Calling the children to duty—
  To the path of virtue and lore.
Hour after hour it called them,
  Singing, " Ding-dong, ding-dong !
To duty, to duty, my children !
  Let duty be ever your song ! "

How often I've heard, how often
  I've laughed at that dear old bell,
As its notes in their glad, wild clearness
  So merrily rose and fell ;
As its ponderous tongue, regardless
  Of making a friend or foe,
Spake out in its fearless accents,
  Unvarying to and fro.
With music the same as ever,
  " To duty, to duty ! " it sang :
" To duty, to duty, my children ! "
  Thus hour after hour it rang.

With joy I retrace my pathway
  Through memory's mazy realm,
Where many glad greetings await me,
  My spirit to overwhelm ;
I revisit the fond old school-house,
  I hear the same music swell,
And I talk with the gray-haired bell-man
  Who faithfully rings the bell,
And the song is the same as ever :
  " To duty, to duty !" it sings ;
" From duty well done in the present
  All future achievement springs !"

THE LOVER'S LAMENT.

I tune my harp 'neath the willows at eve ;
  I tune it to sigh and deplore ;
For alas, alas, it is mine to grieve
  O'er a bliss that is mine no more !
A maiden I loved—O, how madly I loved her !
  And her charms the more radiant beamed
When I sung of my love, and, in singing, so moved her ;
  Then her looks—what a Heaven they seemed !
She smiled her bright smiles which melted my soul,
And I away from myself was stole.
  And I breathed like a spirit that dreamed.

She told me her heart felt the deepest of love,
  And her voice, all music, was such,
It seemed to gush from some lute above,
  Awaked by an angel's touch.
But brief, alas, too brief was my Heaven !
  My bliss all dissolved like a dream.
Her " deepest of love " to another was given ;
  Then her looks, what a hell did they seem !
And now in my sadness this true harp of mine
I tune 'neath the willows at twilight, to pine
  And to sigh forth my plaintive theme.

LOVE AND FANCY.

June's stilly twilight, hazy pale,
Dropped o'er the scenery of the vale,
Thick'ning the shadows of the grove.
There strayed that wondrous spirit, Love,
A princely youth in gay attire,
Rapt 'mid the echoes of his lyre;
And as he stepped his feet kept time
In magic language to the chime,
While his rich voice, now low, now high,
Carolled voluptuous melody,
And at brief intervals the while
Deep grew his sigh and bright his smile;
And fondly he smiled, and fondly he sighed,
He seemed delight personified.

And lo, as he at rapture's height
  In sweet enchantment strayed,
Sudden appeared fair Fancy's sprite—
  A smiling, blushing maid.
Then paused the youth; entranced he stood,
While o'er his cheek and brow a flood
  Of crimson took its way.
The maiden, smiling, blushing still,
Shot with her glance such magic thrill,
  She held him in her sway.

But Love, recovering from the spell,
Felt joy his lips refused to tell—
  A joy known but to such a sprite.
Abashed, yet eager, then he grasped
The maid, and to his bosom clasped
  Her form, so frail and slight,
And in one breath, one sigh, one kiss,
She promised to be ever his;
  Like Heaven was their delight.

Satiate with their ecstatic embrace,
Together they left that enchanted place,
And love, nigh inebriate with delight,
Still pressed to his side that lovely sprite
While on one arm enrapt she clung,
And on the other his wild lyre swung.
And ever since thus, side by side,
In youth and loveliness they glide :
Two sprites were they in time long gone,
But Love and Fancy now are one.

FRIENDSHIP'S TONE AND LAUGH.

Though the bard wakes the string of old friendship so
    much,
  And sings of the banqueting board,
Yet how can I help but to give it a touch
  When my fingers are now on that chord.
When the voice of old years echoes still in my ears,
  And my heart echoes back a response,
And my carol the tone of new friendship endears
  As it laughs out its music at once.

    Blest, blest are the ears that quaff
    Sweet Friendship's Tone and Laugh !
    What a thrilling ring ! O who would not sing
    Of Friendship's Tone and Laugh !

Alas, for the breast that is barren of this,
  A gift which was hallowed above !
For they say that, of old, 'twas an Angel's kiss,
  And it came in the form of a dove :
And believe it, sweet friend, I know it still lives,
  For I hear its fond music in thee ;
In thy bosom it lives, and each note that it gives
  Awakens an echo in me.

    Blest, blest are the ears that quaff, etc., etc.

O sweet the emotion that old friends awake
    When they meet in the real old style ;
When they give to the hand a warm shake for a shake,
    And give a fond smile for a smile :
And when they are met, and the banquet is set,
    And the cups around are given,
And the cheek with a hallowed remembrance is wet,
    Oh what shall I call it but Heaven !

    Blest, blest are the ears that quaff, etc., etc.

CAMPBELL'S LEAP.

A DECLAMATION.

On Campbell's Ledge, at early morn,
Rang out a hunter's echoing horn,
While hoof of steed and hoof of roe
Gave voices to the glen below,
Till every rock and hill around
Flung many an answer to the sound.

But hark ! the notes no longer fly,
Their echoes on the distance die,
Sighing their last without reply.

Fierce frowns the mount in all its pride ;
Lo, half way up its rugged side,
Behold, dismounting from his horse
And bending o'er a deer's red corse,
Campbell, the huntsman of the dale,
Bold Campbell of Wyoming vale.

There silent stands his charger fleet,
Whose rounded form and slender feet
    Tell of his value true.
While bends the huntsman o'er the roe,
And marks how sure has been his bow,
    He hears a wild halloo.

Springing erect, his quick eye spied
Fast clambering up the mountain side
    An Indian swarm, a demon band.
Rapid he glanced from left to right,
Seeking in vain a course for flight ;
    'Twas death to move, 'twas death to stand.

One moment stood he motionless,
As if in doubt, as in distress,
    And 'reft of every hope ;
One moment more his dark eye flashed,
Into the saddle then he dashed
    And galloped 'gainst the slope.

Up, up he struggles, up he climbs,
    His foemen thundering at his heels ;
The footing crumbles, and at times
    He thinks that death e'en now he feels.

Still upward, upward, on he strives :
Sudden he hears the clash of knives,
    And, glancing wildly back,
At one spear's length away he sees
Three of his foremost enemies
    Press hard upon his track,
Striving to wound his noble horse,
Striving to check him in his course ;
    Vain, vain is their attack.

With desperate thought, with desperate strength,
Backward he darts ; and lo, at length,
    He smites the nearest brave,
Who, groaning, flings his arms on high ;
Pale grows his cheek and dim his eye,
    While trembles in his breast the glave.

Yelling a death-yell wild and shrill,
    He grasps his friends in death's own grip ;
Impetuous roll they from the hill ;
Their comrades trample them until

Confusion reigns ; their own they kill,
    And in each other's gore they slip.

Now Campbell, with rekindled hope,
More fiercely speeds against the slope,
    Urging his steed amain.
But O that war-whoop, howl and yell
Too plainly show, too plainly tell
    His foemen come again.

Still keeps he on that deathful track,
And ever and anon looks back,
    Patting his foaming horse.
Still whirl his foemen on behind ;
They seem impelled by fury's wind
    And not by human force.

And well, full well, the huntsman knows
Why such a band, such demon foes
    Are loth to hurl the lance ;
They crave him to glut their fell desire ;
They crave him to glut their hungry fire
    And cheer their brutal dance.

Lo, now the topmost peak they gain !
Nor draws the rider on his rein,
    But plunges headlong still ;
While close behind whirl fierce the foe,
Gaining at every step they go,
    Yelling their war-whoop shrill.

Now skims he 'long the rocky ledge,
And boldly seeks its boldest edge ;
And slumbers fair Wyoming's vale
Full many a fathom there below,
And Susquehanna seems to trail
Like some blue cloud with curving tail.
Yet Campbell, vigorous and hale,
    That dizzy height is scanning now ;
His eye is bright, his cheek is pale,
    A purpose bold is on his brow.

One moment breathes he in the ear
Of his true steed—one moment mere—
And lo that steed, nigh quick as thought.
His four slim feet together brought.

Sudden a dozen warriors grim
　　Dart at the rider there :
Grapple a dozen hands at him.
　　But grapple empty air :
For instant as the lightning's wing
The charger, with a wondrous spring,
　　Is distant like a dart.
Down, down both horse and rider sweep :
Down, down full many a fathom deep,
　　While sick shrinks every heart.

Silent the Red-men stare beneath :
Silent they hold their throbbing breath ;
Silent they quail at such a death.

Still earthward man and charger dash :
Resounding on the stream they crash,
While o'er them foams a towering splash.

They cut the waters like a blade,
　　An instant dart from sight.
　　Bold man, bold beast of might—
Bold man, bold beast, so undismayed—
That was the grandest leap e'er made
　　By Red-man or by White !

But see, O see the river's brim,
　　Where plays the bubbling tide !
A horse and rider struggling swim
　　To gain the further side.

And now they reach the verdant shore ;
　　Bold Campbell smiles again.
Fondles his charger o'er and o'er.
　　Stroking his silky mane.
He mounts the saddle as before
　　And homeward turns his rein.

No man was happier, none more gay
In all the vale for many a day,
As told and retold he the tale
To trembling wife and children pale.

Wyoming cried, with lips aflame,
" Would ye extol bold Campbell's fame ?
Give to the ledge bold Campbell's name."

ADIEU, TILL WE MEET AGAIN.

TO ANNA.

O love ! you rosebud late kissed by the dews
   Transcendant in beauty seems ;
But O, thy cheeks, as thy teardrops suffuse,
   Far richer in loveliness beams.
That snow white arm, and that snow white hand,
   Such eyes, and such glances, too !
Forgive me, but O, as you weeping stand,
My soul is tempted beyond command,
To repeat that fond adieu.
Then adieu, adieu ! my love, adieu !
   Let thy bosom be free from pain ;
For, when distant I rove, I'll be true to my love ;
   Adieu, till we meet again !

The song of you oriole, O, my love !
   Seems matchless, so rich and clear ;
But O, thy words are like notes from above,
   And not like the sounds from our sphere.
'Tis heaven to feel thine enchanting sways,
   As thy hair like the sunbeam flows,
And thy snowy neck gleams through that ringlet maze,
And thy blue eyes beam forth such a wishful gaze,
And thy cheek with love's ardor glows :
Then adieu, adieu ! my love, adieu !
   Still my hopes all with thee remain ;
And though distant I rove, I shall think of my love ;
   Adieu, till we meet again !

O SWEET THE DREAM OF BYGONE DAYS.

STANZAS FOR MUSIC.

O sweet the dream of bygone days,
　　When, with a fond regret,
The soul looks back through memory's maze
　　To scenes bright even yet;
Bright even to the hoary head
　　Long since bowed low in grief;
But oft 'mid thoughts of pleasures fled
　　The lorn soul finds relief.

　　O sweet the dream of bygone days,
　　　　Of hearts that loving met;
　　Such joy, such love, such magic sways,
　　　　Ah! can I e'er forget?

Fond, fond the thoughts of early joy,
　　Of youth's intense delight,
The blushing girl, the laughing boy,
　　Their faces radiant bright,
The full eyes beaming forth the soul,
　　The breasts that wildly loved,
The smile that played, the glance that stole,
　　Which matrons would reprove.

　　O sweet the dream, etc., etc.

O sweet the dream of past delight,
　　When youths roamed o'er the green,
And lovers gave their fond, fond plight
　　In nook and bower serene.
Like roses blushing in the sun
　　Those scenes did then invite me;
Like scents of roses that are gone,
　　Now thoughts of them delight me.

　　O sweet the dream, etc., etc.

SONG OF PARTING COMPANIONS.

O comrades, fond and true,
Come let me drink to you ;
Perhaps that day is far away
  When we may pledge anew :
Then let us quaff with merry laugh,
  And merry hand-shake, too.

When we are wide apart,
Still hold we in our heart
The fond farewell our lips now tell,
  Our friendship, free of art :
When memories trace each friendly face,
  Check not the tears that start.

O comrades, fond and true,
Come let me drink to you :
Yea, pledge we here, with smile and tear,
  And hearty hand-shake, too.
And now be heard that sighful word,
  Adieu, a long adieu.

MIDNIGHT VISIONS.

The midnight moments creep ;
  Fond visions rise before me,
And, as I long to sleep,
  Thrill after thrill steals o'er me ;
I see the friends that memory sends,
  I gaze upon their faces,
And lo, my love ! now blest above,
  Awaits my warm embraces.
The midnight moments creep ;
  The vision smiles before me ;
I can not, can not sleep,
  A joyful thrill steals o'er me.

How rare those eyes of blue !
   Those flowing golden tresses !
How sweet the kisses too !
   How tender the caresses !
O when she wept for joy, then slept
   Upon my heaving bosom,
I watched her keep that placid sleep,
   Breathing like some fair blossom.
The golden moments sweep :
   The vision glows before me :
I will not, will not sleep :
   A blissful thrill steals o'er me.

The joyful moments sweep,
   And forms of those that love me,
With smiles, delay my sleep,
   One hovers close above me.
O that my love, now blest above,
   Could dart to me this even,
With fond caress my lips to bless !
   I'd crave no more from Heaven.
The solemn moments creep,
   The phantom flits before me,
And as I fain would sleep,
   A saddening thrill steals o'er me.

TO ANNA.

O Anna, fond Anna, recall you the pain
   Of our parting, when bitter you wept,
When vowed I devotion till met we again ?
   O that vow, that sweet promise, I've kept !

Kind hearts have I met, on my wandering way
   And I've basked in the smiles of the fair ;
But believe me, my Anna, I could not be gay,
   For no Anna, no Anna was there.

But now I'm restored to the star of my dream,
  To leave thee, to leave thee no more ;
Again let thy sunny smiles over me beam ;
  Come smile, Anna, smile as of yore.

O now am I blest, for my star is afire
  With a flame from a heavenlier sphere ;
How exquisite ! but ah, it will some time expire !
  My bliss will be transient I fear !

But here's to my Anna, the pride of her dale,
  Whatever betide her and me :
O, if these were the last drops of wine in our vale,
  I would quaff them, sweet Anna, to thee !

ANNA.

Long years have passed since Anna,
  My bride, my lovely Fay,
Gave me her hand forever—
  All joyful was that day.
O how we loved each other !
  Our love was more than love :
We loved with such an ardor
  As angels might above.
When oft I sighed all trembling,
  "O love, wert thou to die,
How could I breathe without thee,"
  She'd answer with a sigh,
"Then let these words of Anna
  Console thee to thy fate :
Take heart, take heart, she waits thee
  Within the golden gate."

Long years have passed since Anna,
  My bride, my lovely Fay,
Drooped like a broken lily—
  All woeful was that day !

I watched her as she suffered,
    A flush was on her cheek,
I saw her eyes grow dimmer,
    I heard her voice grow weak;
Then left her cheek the rosebud,
    The lovelight left her eye :
Then fled her smiles—O, heaven !
    I saw my Anna die !
Yet though my fate be bitter,
    These words my soul elate :
" Take heart, take heart, she waits thee
    Within the golden gate."

THEY SAY THAT THE FAIRIES HAVE POWER.

TO ANNA.

They say that the fairies have power
    To do the most marvelous things—
Change a babe or a maid to a flower,
    Or give them invisible wings.

And the fairies are lovers of graces,
    For they have been angels of yore :
So they choose but the loveliest faces
    To enflower or wing evermore.

O thou wert so lovely, my Anna,
    I can not believe thou hast died,
But that fairies from old Lackawanna
    Have taken thee there to reside.

Still I know they've not given thee wings, love,
    For then thou would'st surely be here :
But I can not conceive the strange things, love !
    To what rose could they change one so dear ?

I'll away to the old Lackawanna,
    Where fairest the roses are now ;
And the loveliest flower, sweet Anna,
    I'll seek, for I know 'twill be thou !

FRIENDSHIP'S CHAIN.

SUNG AT A BANQUET HELD BY PARTING CLASSMATES.

Ah, little thought we, when at first
    We met as strangers, face to face,
That friendship's chain, in time, might burst
    With parting sigh, with last embrace.
With sigh and with embrace may part
    That chain whose links now round us wind ;
But dead the soul and dead the heart,
    That such links can not always bind.

CHORUS :

What heart shall not a rapture feel,
    What breast shall not know sweet regret,
When school-day memories o'er them steel ?
    Such time, such joy, can we forget ?

Can we forget or cease to think
    Of all, of each with whom we've played ?
Has friendship's chain so slight a link
    That distance cuts it with her blade ?
No, no ! Dame Nature kind has cast
    For us a chain which ever winds ;
So presence holds us firm and fast,
    And absence but more closely binds.

Cho.—What heart shall not a rapture feel, etc., etc.

Can we forget this happy time,
    Each happy voice we hear to-night ?
Ah, to the one who sings this rhyme,
    Mere thoughts of them will be delight.
Then give the toast ; let each one drink,
    E'en though the cup be not of red :
O never may old friendship's link
    Desert our hearts, benumbed and dead !

Cho.—What heart shall not a rapture feel, etc., etc.

TO CLEMATIS,

ON HIS THIRTEENTH BIRTHDAY.

Clematis, e'en though we are severed afar,
  And 'twere idle to wish thou wert here,
Yet my thoughts, like the rays from a distant star,
  May reach thee and make thee seem near.

When thou know'st my thoughts, when thou feel'st their
      thrill,
  If such there be in my rhyme,
Thou wilt know that an absent heart loves thee still,
  And blesses thy birthday time.

I miss thy bright smile and thy sigh so fond,
  And I miss thy fond words, fonder still,
Touched into flame by some fairy wand ;
  That wand, call it love if you will.

Yet, love, can it be ?   Did I say, call it love ?
  Yes, such is the music I said ;
For love is a note sung by angels above,
  And the soul that ne'er heeds it is dead.

Now send, I pray, ere thy birthday glides by,
  A fond wish, a fond sigh to me ;
For I this day send many a sigh
  And many a wish to thee.

Clematis, Clematis, my buxom lad,
  Laugh, laugh thy loudest to-day ;
And to thee may there never be morrow more sad,
  And never a morrow less gay.

SONG TO THE BUTTERCUP.

Sweet buttercup, which gazeth up
  With nods and smiles and golden brightness,
There live in me fond thoughts of thee
  Which lift my heart to gladsome lightness ;
E'er bloom and flourish pretty little flower ;
Live on and smile in sunshine and in shower.

Thou art a sprite of pure delight,
  For plant thou dost but slight resemble ;
Thy petals show a heavenly glow
  When wind and sunbeam make thee tremble ;
O bloom and brighten, gladden every hour ;
Yea, gaily smile in sunshine and in shower.

How oft I took thee near the brook !
  It gave me joy no words could utter
To have thee shine beneath my chin,
  And tell my mates if liked I butter :
Still bloom and charm the schoolboy in his bower ;
Still fondly smile in sunshine and in shower.

Thy tiny face with look of grace
  Invites the children's lips to kiss thee ;
Let girl and boy drink deep thy joy,
  For days may come when they shall miss thee ;
Bloom, ever bloom, thou pretty little flower ;
Still smile thy smiles in sunshine and in shower.

O WHERE IS THE BLOOM THAT BLUSHED.

TO GLYCERA.

O where is the bloom that blushed
  On thy cheek, sweet Glycera, my own ?
And where is the voice that hushed
  My heart with its magic of tone ?
And where are the eyes that glanced
  A rapture in every look ?
And where are the smiles that danced,
  And the sighs which the zephyrs took ?
All are flown ; and the snow that drifts
  Is their winding-sheet—too rude ;
They fled like the rainbow gifts
  Which together in childhood we viewed.
But where, my Glycera, Oh where
  Art thou, my sweet day-dream of yore ?
My infancy knew thee, too fair ;
  But alas, I can know thee no more !

I revisit our snow-covered bowers,
　　And thy grave 'neath the willows I find ;
Thou hast faded away like the flowers
　　Which together in childhood we twined !

SONNET TO THE OLD YEAR.

Farewell to thee, farewell, departing year :
　　In gloom I watch thy final hours descend,
　　And mourn thee as I should a bosom friend.
With saddened heart, with sigh and flowing tear.
We mortals pause to contemplate in fear,
For O, our record closes with thy end—
A record which we never more may mend—
　　Deeds, good and evil, sleep upon the bier.
Farewell to thee, once more a last farewell—
　　Hark ! art thou vanished ?　And for ever too ?
Ay, thou art flown, I hear thy funeral knell !
　　I've but one thought and that's to start anew
With spotless record and to persevere
In living well through all the glad new year.

SONNET TO F. B.

O friend, 'tis joy e'en to the mind depressed
To meet once more a friend's bright smiling face,
When hands grasp warm, and arms too interlace,
And wildly glad the heart swells forth the breast.
When loving soul by loving soul is blest,
The hours on wings of joy each other chase ;
'Tis so when schoolboys meet in fond embrace :
Of happy times this is the happiest.
But ah, my friend, though sweet, 'tis sad to think
　　So many friends are ours, nor false is any :
'Tis sweet that all these hearts with ours now link ;
　　'Tis sad that some day we must lose so many :
Yet laugh we on, while laugh our glad hearts may,
Let doubt and sadness follow yesterday.

SONG OF CUPID.

O fill up the cups with a sparkling wine,
And drink with glad hearts to this music of mine !
For mine is the magic that flavors the draught,
And renders it sweeter than aught ever quaffed ;
I touch but a chord and the notes fly in sweetness,
And fill the red goblet with odors exquisite,
And lend to Time's wings a magical fleetness,
And form a new realm which the soul may revisit.
O if there be magic more wondrous than mine,
　　Where is it ?　Where is it ?

O mine are the songs that enchant the fair
With their ravishing charms, all their talents rare,
Who, though they be cold as the dews of night,
Must melt at my notes into Love's delight.
And mine are the lays that sustain the spirit ;
Their spells from the strength of the airs they elicit,
To charm the red wine cup, that those who revere it
May revel in ecstasy's trance when they kiss it.
O if there be magic more wondrous than mine,
　　Where is it ?　Where is it ?

GULA AND LILY AND NET.

Three little children come running,
　Gula and Lily and Net ;
On to my knees they scramble ;
　Which do you think is my pet ?

Gula, a sweet little rose-bud,
　Sits prattling now on my knee,
So free with her smiles and her kisses ;
　Do you think that my choicest is she ?

My other knee holds my fond Lily,
　Fond as that beautiful flower,
And with kisses and smiles she caresses ;
　Think you she is my star of the hour ?

With her arms round my neck soft entwining
  Is Net, whom " Fair Blossom " I call,
Just as free with her smiles and her kisses ;
  Think you she is the dearest of all ?

I've a rose-bud, a lily, a blossom,
  Pinned side by side on my breast ;
These three are my choicest of flowers ;
  Which is the sweetest and best ?

I am loved by three little children—
  Gula and Lily and Net—
And each do I love as dearly,
  And each do I claim as my pet.

But think, little girls, a few summers
  May see you to womanhood grow,
And me to a crusty old bachelor ;
  Will your smiles to my kisses then glow ?

MINEPHTHAH.

A FRAGMENT.

Of Egyptian Minephthah O have ye not heard,
  Who, content with the deeds he had done,
Full sudden expired, and flew off like a bird,
  To dwell in the bark of the sun !

FATHER OF THE NIGHT AND MORN.

A HYMN.

Father of the night and morn,
From whose breath all life is born,
Spirit present everywhere,
O vouchsafe to hear my prayer ;
Hear a prayer, whose every word
Flames up from a heart that erred ;
Erred, ay erred, though it could see
Worlds lit by Thy deity.

I have strayed, a willful child,
On life's pathway, bleak and wild ;
Urged on step by step to tread,
By the hope of joy ahead,
Heedless of Thy signs and wonders
Shown in lightnings or in thunders,
Till, o'erwhelmed, I turned to Thee,
Hailed Thy vast ubiquity.

Now repentant kneel I here,
That my sorrow's moan and tear
Might secure me respite blest
From the pangs which rend my breast.
O may He, who died to save
Souls from death, may He who gave
Life to dead, made blind men see,
May He grant some grace to me.

QUARREL OF BRUTUS AND CASSIUS.

A DIALOGUE FOR BOYS.

Cassius.—That thou hast wronged me is too clear,
For I have paid the forfeit dear ;
My teacher smacked me well.
Yea, like the dickens did he smack !
Tore the suspenders from my back—
The rest I blush to tell.
But all this smacking borne by me,
False Brutus, hath been caused by thee.

Brutus.—Nay, thou hast brought thyself the blame,
And now, sly Cassius, bear the shame ;
And here I tell thee true,
After the burning of the spellers,
I heard thee whisper 'mong the fellers ;
The teacher heard thee, too.

Cas.—'Tis false, 'tis false, thou Nannygoat !
        Thou know'st thou liest in thy throat,
            For thou didst me betray !
        And Brutus, it is not but once
        That thou hast proved thyself a dunce,
            And given a trick away.

Bru.—What ! I a dunce ? Hold, hold thy tongue,
        Or, by my troth, though I'll be hung,
            I'll teach thee what to say.

Cas.—Ha ! teach thy betters what to say ?
        Learn first thyself from me, I pray,
            But treason thou can'st teach :
        Yet if again thou squeal'st on me,
        By all that is or e'er shall be,
            That moment thou shalt bleach !

Bru.—Platonian goose without a feather !
        Thou parrot with a pate of leather,
            I fear thee not one bit !

Cas.—Thou bean of old Pythagoras !
        Thou sneakest like a snake in grass,
            But thou shalt pay for it !

Bru.—Thy threats in me no terror find !
        They pass me as the idle wind
            Which buzzes past my brow :
        Yet, lackaday ! that I should brook
        A threatening word or threatening look
            From such a child as thou.
        I say I'm thy superior !

Cas.—Superior in treason's lore,
            And tell-tale too, I trow.

Bru.—Ha ! now thy tongue doth wag a joke,
        With pointed dart and pointed poke,
            But's all the same to me.

Cas.—Then, Brutus, let us make amends ;
    Let's join our hands again as friends.

Bru.—I'll differ not with thee ;
    But here's my heart and here's my hand,
    And by each other shall we stand
       In fight or trickery.

Cas.—Dost thou agree so much indeed ?
    Full glad am I such words to heed ;
      With joy my heart is flamed.
    But, Brutus, what caused us to quarrel,
    Like girls to scream, like dogs to snarl ?
      For my part I'm ashamed.

Bru.—Well, by my troth, I scarce know what.
    There was no cause, else I've forgot—
      There's no one to be blamed.

Cas. —In sooth I know not, but, methinks,
    'Twas caused by smiles or bitter winks,
      We've cast upon each other.

Bru. —True, true, a likely cause, indeed !
    A smile or wink oft proves a seed
      Which sprouts a tree of bother.

Cas.—And strange the time our bother sprung,
    When school-day carol should be sung,
    And dialogues should be rehearsed,
    And school-time secrets should be nursed,
    And—

Bru. —Nay, hold, I pray, O Cassius, hold !
    'Tis passed ; our quarrel's already cold.
    Then pledge we friendship as of yore,
    But this time pledge for evermore ;
    Let's stand like brother by a brother,
    Yea, play or fight beside each other.

THE CHIEFTAIN AND HIS BARD.

By Susquehanna sat two Indian braves,
Where hemlocks' shadow made them darker still.
The one was silent, but his eyes, the while,
Flashed forth a language from a soul afire.
Those eyes it was, as well as that tall frame
Of might and grace, that crowned him, as he was,
The mightiest chieftain of Wyoming vale.

The other close resembled him in form,
But wore a milder mien and gentler grace :
His dark eyes, too, flamed fire, but subtler fire,
Which spake of song and dream and mystery.

Within his hands was clasped an instrument,
Of rude construction, but of music's voice,
Which followed up in sweetness his discourse,
In chant, in war-hymn, or in prophecy.
And now his notes soft tremble through the air,
As thus before his mighty chief he sings :

"O Talakeena, time was when my voice
Could tell of joy and love in merry strain,
Stealing its tunes from bird and breeze and brook :
But now, alas! it takes its flight, half winged,
Humming, perforce, the hemlock's tone and tune,
That dismal moaning of the wind and burs.

"E'en like the north wind am I doomed to plain,
A restless spirit, nowhere finding rest ;
And now, O Talakeena, do not frown
If once again I speak of mystery.

"In dream I heard the war-whoop of our tribe ;
From mount to distant mount it echoed wild,
And all Wyoming rushed at once to arms.
Quick to the front swept Talakeena bold,
Fierce as the east wind, when its breath is sharp ;
And every brave saw vengeance on his brow.

" Lo, down fair Susquehanna like a tempest
Thundered amain a race of strange, strange beings,
White as the north-wind's fleece, when the wild waves
Of Lackawanna stiffen and are mute.

" Then clashed a conflict, equalled ne'er before.
The foemen met our charge with mighty knives,
Which clove our braves in twain ; still hope was ours,
Till suddenly, the big white chieftain placed,
A long pipe in his mouth, as if to smoke,
Which gave a scream like to a wounded hawk,
Half music, and half like a brave's death-yell.
Then, like the broken fires from the great Spirit,
When rages he in fury 'gainst his children,
There hurled upon us flame and smoke and thunder.

" Then was it that we quailed ; for well we knew
Our foemen held the lightnings in their hands,
And held the thunderbolts, and powers unknown.

" Our tribe lay strewn like grass beneath a flood,
And lo ! O now, great Manito, now comes
A scene more dire than death itself—O chief,
O Talakeena, thee I saw alone,
There on the bloody hillside, bleeding, bleeding,
Bleeding from head to foot through countless wounds,
Still pressed at bay, e'en as a hunted stag !
I shrieked—I shrieked ! and shrieking I awoke."
The minstrel ceased ; but ere his echoes died,
The chieftain rising to his feet began :

" Alkrane, sweet singer, Alkrane, O my bard,
Grieve not for Talakeena and his braves.
That foe breathes not, whom he or they shall fear ;
For they and he are of Wyoming birth.
Our fathers died ; we are our fathers' sons ;
And shall we not meet death as bold as they ?

" But if we fall, Wyoming, fare thee well !
Farewell, ye mountains, forests, and ye hills,

And Lackawanna's wild and laughing stream,
And Susquehanna, Manito's great flood,
Farewell, farewell, be this our last farewell !
For O who knows but that we may be lost
Ere we can frame that burning word again."

So spake great Talakeena ; and his breast
Now heaved a long-drawn sigh. He waved his hand
At Alkrane to arise ; then chief and bard
In silence and in sadness, side by side,
Glided into the forest's deepest shades.

"BREAK, BREAK, BREAK!"

SUGGESTED BY ALFRED TENNYSON'S POEM OF THE SAME TITLE.

O bright was the blush of the morning,
    And bright was the smile on the wave,
But sad, ah, sad was the minstrel,
    And sad was the song that he gave.
Alone on the beach did he wander,
    Alone on the beach strayed he,
And aye and anon, as the waves rolled on,
    He gazed far over the sea.

Still the waves rolled on, and aye and anon,
    As he heard each new echo awake,
He sighed, ah, he sighed in his plaintive lay,
    "Roll on, roll on for aye and for aye!"
    And "break, break, break!"

Then turned he his glance to the rearward,
    To a boy with his sister at play ;
And thence to a distant sailor,
    Who merrily warbled his lay ;
Then sad and more sad sighed the minstrel,
    And sad and more sad rose his strain,
Whilst aye and anon, as the waves rolled on,
    He gazed far over the main.

Still the waves rolled on, and aye and anon,
    As he heard each new echo awake,
He sighed, ah, he sighed in his plaintive lay,—
" Roll on, roll on for aye and for aye ! "
    And "break, break, break !"

He sung of a day gone for ever,
    And he wept as he uttered the thought ;
He wept, yes, he wept o'er an image
    Deep, deep at his heart's core wrought :
And he sung of a voice that is silent,
    Mid sighs and mid tear-drops sung he,
Whilst aye and anon, as the waves rolled on,
    He gazed far over the sea.

Still the waves rolled on ; and aye and anon,
    As he heard each new echo awake,
He sighed, ah, he sighed in that plaintive lay—
" Roll on, roll on for aye and for aye ! "
    And " break, break, break ! "

THE GRIEF OF AVOCA.

O bright was the smile by Avoca worn,
Bright as the sun of that joyful morn ;
And Avoca's own children waxed merry and gay
As the moments, all golden, sped laughing away ;
And the words of the brave, and the looks of the fair
Told how the spirit of pleasure reigned there ;
But though radiant that morn with its promises fond,
O well for Avoca had never it dawned.

Away swept the throng, that holiday throng,
While their hearts were made merry by laughter and song ;
Ah, they seemed like the bubbles upon the wave,
Reveling over the brink of the grave,
Which glitter and glide in their gladsome excess,
Till sudden they're dashed into nothingness ;

Or e'en like some flowers which at morn are in bloom,
But at eventide wither, and sink in their tomb.
Such, such, alas, O such was the fate
Of the sons of Avoca, so desolate.

That eventide spread her dark wings on the gale,
And flew, like the angel of death, o'er the vale ;
O'er the vale of Avoca she flew in her gloom,
Her wing but a shroud, and her body a tomb ;
And the autumn winds wailed, and the autumn winds
    groaned,
While new widows and orphans their loved ones be-
    moaned ;
Still the autumn winds groaned and the autumn winds
    wailed,
While parents and brothers and sisters all quailed.
Then deeply, alas ! did Avoca deplore !
Then, then did she weep as she ne'er wept before !
And the winds of the autumn still wail there and moan ;
And Avoca mourns, too, o'er the souls that are flown.

SPRING SMILES AGAIN.

THOUGHTS OF ANNA.

Spring smiles again in revel gay,
    Yet, 'neath that smile so glad,
I see a death, a by-gone day,
    And my heart grows lorn and sad.

Again I wander by the trees,
    Where, oft in times gone by,
I heard love sighed in every breeze,
    And I gave back sigh for sigh.

The lark sang love with wanton tongue,
    The rose-bud sang it, too :
Ah, me ! it seems that love was sung
    By every sound that flew.

A happy time, a happy time !
  How blest each eventide,
When wooed I in a quaint love-rhyme
  The dear one at my side.

Then waxed her charms more bright, her smile
  So fond, her voice so fine ;
And what delight to press, the while,
  Her thrilling hand in mine !

Her silence spell-bound music seemed ;
  And when she broke the spell
Her tones upon my heart, I deemed,
  Like honeyed dew-drops fell.

But fleet, too fleet those evenings !
  Each gave its bliss and passed
Away—away on fairy wings--
  Oh could it always last !

Alas, we had to part ! O heaven,
  That was a trying minute !
O why was power to love so given,
  To have such magic in it ?

I will not, O I will not paint
  That scene ; for fast and fast
My heart would throb, and failing paint ;
  That parting was our last !

That parting was our last ; and yet,
  Though knew I that too well,
I haunted still where we had met,
  And why I scarce could tell.

The lark sung love with wanton tongue,
  But O the pain it gave !
Of love the breeze and rose-bud sung :
  I heard them but to rave.

'Twas love that every sound still sang,
  But O, how changed was I !
For each note turned into a pang,
  And into a moan each sigh.

Yet when spring time died away,
    And leafy June did wither,
Though all things fair seemed to decay,
    Still strayed my footsteps thither.

A joyless time, a joyless time,
    Had I for months and years ;
Even now at times the quaint love rhyme
    Still echoes in my ears.

And when fair spring is reveling gay
    Beneath her smile so glad,
I see a death, a by-gone day,
    And my heart grows lorn and sad.

TO CLEMATIS.

Clematis, Clematis, my song is to thee !
To Clematis I sing, and my heart sings to me,
And none but Clematis sighs love to me now,
And none has such sighs, my Clematis, as thou.
'Tis Clematis that cheers me when deep I despond ;
'Tis Clematis that smiles me to happiness fond ;
'Tis he that loves true, and 'tis he that loves free ;
O, 'tis he and his love that are ever with me.
Clematis, Clematis, my song is to thee !
To Clematis I sing, and my heart sings to me.

How oft have I asked, " Is there under the sun
One heart that is constant—aye, is there e'en one
Which in friendship or love can be true to the last ? "
Nay, hold, my dear boy ! do not redden so fast !
For when I met thee all my doubts were o'erthrown,
And my confidence poured just as free as thine own ;
And were I to tell what bliss gladdens my brow,
I should say, my Clematis, that blessing is thou.
Clematis, Clematis, my song is to thee ;
To Clematis I sing, and my heart sings to me.

Away with the smile and the kiss of the fair,
For that smile is deceit and that kiss is a snare ;
But give me the frank-hearted school-boy, a friend
That loves like Clematis, who loves to the end.
'Tis Clematis that cheers me, when deep I despond ;
'Tis Clematis that laughs me to happiness fond ;
And 'tis he that loves true, and 'tis he that loves free ;
O, 'tis he and his love that are ever with me.
Clematis, Clematis, my song is to thee !
To Clematis I sing, and my heart sings to me.

TO CLEMATIS.

Months—years, have passed, Clematis, since we met,
　Since first I kissed thy boyish tear away,
　And taught thy heart to feel true friendship's sway ;
But that sweet tutoring do I now regret ?
　The task was easy, both to teach and learn ;
　I gave thee love, thou loved'st in return.

The moment that thy thrilling hand pressed mine
　I felt that we had met and loved before,
And that our hearts, impelled by power divine,
　Each other sought, to live old friendship o'er ;
Ah, yes ! the treasure which I then acquired
Seemed one my secret heart had long desired.

In me at once thy confidence was placed,
　And mine in thee ; fast friends we were e'en then.
How sweet that hour when met we and embraced ;
　How sad it seemed when parted we again ;
Yet I was glad, for, at the parting touch,
Delight was mine to feel beloved so much.

When oft thy feet came tripping to my door,
　How fondly beat my heart to welcome thee ;
And when thou wouldst rehearse thy troubles o'er,
　The chance to soothe thee was a joy to me.
Aught in my power could I refuse to do
For thee, and thou a friend so good, so true ?

Whene'er I smiled, thy face beamed happiness ;
　Whene'er I sighed, sad, too, throbbed thy fond heart ;
Whene'er I grieved, thine eyes wept keen distress ;
　And this, all this so pure and free of art.
Since thou, sweet friend, art constant soul to me,
How else than constant can I be to thee ?

CHRISTMAS BELL.

A HYMN.

Ring out !　Ring out, O Christmas bell !
　Peal forth in merry chime !
Let sound and echo wildly tell
　The glory of the time !

The birth of our Redeemer sing,
　And sing in meetest strain,
And let His name and fame take wing
　O'er mountain, stream and plain.

Sing of the child, our Prince, our Guide,
　Who came in swaddling clothes ;
Sing how He lived, sing how He died,
　And how from death He rose.

Then let the melting music float,
　Resounding through the air ;
Yea, let the wildness from thy throat
　Pour gladness everywhere.

Be this a day of praise and rest,
　All free of worldly care ;
" Come, all ye faithful," hail the blest
　With music and with prayer.

And ring, O Christmas bell, to Him,
　Cause of our ecstasy,
Whom Cherubim, and Seraphim
　Adore on bended knee.

IS HE DEAD?

WRITTEN FOR MRS. R. WHOSE SON, A SCHOOL-MATE OF
THE AUTHOR, DIED WHILE AT SCHOOL.

They tell me he's dead !   But can I believe ?
Can this be the grief that a mother must grieve ?
Or is it some nightmare in which I thus start,
While smothers my breast, and while shudders my heart?
But yesterday, O, and my boy, fondest one,
I beheld, as he smiled, in my fanciful dream ;
This moment, alas ! how his bloom is all gone !
No color, no smiles on his placid face beam ;
But the paleness of death is upon it instead !
Yet can it be death ?   Is he dead ?   Is he dead ?

But stir, oh, my loved one, those lips, wan and pale !
But stir them, and breathe a response to my wail !
Frame even the shape of one kiss for a kiss !
Kind Heaven O grant me—O grant me but this !
Still fixed are his eyes, still mute is his tongue ;
Still smileless his face, and still heedless his ear ;
Nor feels he the bosom to which he hath clung,
Nor heeds he the tears which fall fast on his bier !
Alas, he's no more !   His bright spirit is fled !
Yet can it be death ?   Is he dead ?   Is he dead ?

Good bye, ah, my lost one, a final good bye ;
Yet another fond kiss, and another fond sigh ;
And now let those cold, palid lips of thine
Press a lasting, a lasting farewell upon mine ;
But oh, can it be that forever we part ?
Can it be that forever I'm left in despair?
Nay, again may we meet in that realm where thou art ;
And a smile and embrace wilt thou have for me there,
Where grief is unknown, where never is said,—
" O can it be death ?   Is he dead ?   Is he dead ?"

ALKRANE'S SONG.

Fondest scene, the rarest
   Vision in the land,
Full of life, the fairest
   Works of Nature's hand ;
Full of life and beauty,
Full of enchanting sways,
   The touches, here and there, of fairy wand.

The pine tree whispers back my sigh,
The willow tosses it on high,
The zephyr wafts it to the sky :
And there it echoes, but to die.
The hemlock sobs in utter gloom,
And warns me of a direful doom ;
A doom, a doom, a direful doom,
Warns me of a direful doom.

Mine is a fate as dark as night,
Dark as the crow on yonder height :
I shoot my arrow, and lo, he's dead !
So I shall die in a stream of red.
The sturdy oak of strength and power
   Is shattered by the tempest's hand ;
So I shall drop in some future hour,
   Beneath the downfall of our land.
O mine are the dreams that fates destroy,
And mine are thoughts of a vacant joy,
A joy that smiles like the summer's charm,
Which ends its calm in a thunder storm.
Yea, the dreams that live in my idle mind
   Grow, like the bubbles that effervesce,
Which reflect the scenery left behind,
   Then fly into empty nothingness.
The bubbles are burst by a puff of breath,
In a moment the dreams are vanished in death.
We are the bubbles upon the wave,
And we are the dreams above the grave.

Let but a gush of air blow nigh,
  And we, the bubbles, are no more ;
Let but a moment's vision die,
  And we, the dreams, to oblivion soar.
The bubbles and dreams are alike in worth,
As reflections or shadows upon the earth—
Reflections and shadows, uncertain things—
Fanned from existence by others' wings.
A foe is the treacherous puff of wind
  That wreaks the bubbles' sudden doom ;
And a foe is the whirlwind of the mind
  That sweeps the dreams into utter gloom.

All, all are but dreams, for a time to abide,
And all are but bubbles upon the tide.
Such is our grief or happiness,
And such is our pleasure or distress.
The whirlwind might rise and sweep us away ;
  Our fate, our destruction none, none would deplore ;
The waters might rush in their fierceness of play,
  And hurl us at once to eternity's shore.

O ours is a fate that is yet unknown,
But the music of hope is already flown.
The eagle may hide in his rocky eyrie ;
In his covert the panther may crouch, wild and fiery ;
But I, alas I, my kindred and I,
  Are destined to drink of the hemlock's blood,
To rave like the starved wolf, to famish and die,
  Without even a grave in our own native wood.

      On Time's rapid river,
        In our frail canoe,
      We shall conquer never,
        We are but a few.
      Should we strive not hand in hand,
      Woe shall be our native land,
        And our honor too.

The scene about me still is fair,
    A smile lights up her face :
She even laughs as I despair
    The downfall of our race.

The pine tree whispers back my sigh,
The willow tosses it on high,
Zephyrs waft it to the sky,
And there it echoes, but to die.
The hemlock sobs in utter gloom,
And warns me of a direful doom ;
A doom, a doom, a direful doom,
And warns me of a direful doom.

AUTUMN IN PREHISTORIC WYOMING.

Autumn, clad in her melancholy robe
Of mellow dreariness, dark frowned and sighed,
Causing a universal groan and sob ;
And nature's tattered garments wild did ride,
Piece after piece, upon the wind ; the dried
And withered leaves behind the trees were heaped,
Checked in their chase on the aerial tide,
Within whose depths the yellow sunshine peeped :
And bright from scene to scene its flashes danced and
    leaped.

Many a flower was falling to decay :
The mosses gathered round the lifeless brush ;
The grasshopper, in chilly suit of gray,
Perched on a time-worn rock or dying bush,
And chirped a sad complaint unto the thrush ;
Uttered and chirped it in a plaintive tone,
Intreating the golden-rod its grief to hush ;
Yet begged the sunflower, by the stream, to moan
With him, and not to flee, and let him grieve alone.

The woodchuck stood, a sentinel, at the hole,
A blinking sentinel that fain would sleep.

Now forth a pace or two he softly stole,
Then back, with lazy step, his watch to keep.
The cauquaw, the quilled porcupine, would leap
Among the hemlock branches in the dark,
Losing his prickly armor ; thence, 'twould leap
From tree to tree, stripping them of their bark,
Leaving throughout the forest his destructive mark.

The crow soared to the pine-tree's lofty top,
Cawing and croaking to his fellow bird :
Cawing and croaking without change or stop,
Till dismal echoes through the gloom were heard.
The catbird winged his shadowy flight, and blurred
The hazy daylight with his wings and tail,
Deep'ning the gloomness with his song absurd,
Which mocked itself, and proved a piteous wail ;
He flew, companionless, throughout the wooded vale.

SCENE IN PREHISTORIC WYOMING.

Amidst a wild and beauteous scene,
Where verdure was of richest green,
And loudest sang the rippling rills
Between the thickly wooded hills,
Bold Talakeena forth did ride,
With many an Indian at his side,
Galloping on with spirit gay,
To drink the pleasure of the day.

They scampered over dale and hill,
Far down the valley, calm and still :
Sometimes on Susquehanna's side,
Sometimes upon the upland wide ;
Holding aloft the brandished spear
To smite the fleet affrighted deer,
And struggling fierce to keep apace
With Talakeena in the chase.

On, on they dashed, at break-neck speed ;
Each rider lashed his fiery steed,
And volleyed forth shrill whoops and yells
Which echoed through the distant dells,
Putting to flight the deer or hare
That crept dismayed for refuge there.

A LACKAWANNA LEGEND.

At mid-day an Indian maiden stood,
Sighing to fair Lackawanna's flood,
Where a poplar drooped over the river's edge,
The trysting place of her secret pledge.
Now over the waters her glance she swept,
    And now behind her, as if afraid,
And then by turns she smiled and wept,
    Then gazed on the waves as they danced and played :
But the waves still danced, and the waves still played,
Like the fancies and hopes of the beautiful maid.

Lo ! sudden is seen on the waters blue
A warrior bold in a birchen canoe ;
When soon on the flower-spangled bank he stepped,
The maiden smiled, and the maiden wept.
Enraptured she flew to her lover's arms,
    Nor thought of the sire whom she disobeyed ;
Each, stolen from self by the other's charms,
    Heard not the waves as they danced and played :
But the waves still danced, and the waves still played,
As fluttered the hearts of the youth and the maid.

Again the bold warrior sought his canoe,
And soon was afar on the waters blue.
Alas, alas ! the sweetest bliss
Oft comes and goes like a lover's kiss !
The youth to his battles away was gone,
    To fall, perhaps, by the foeman's blade ;

And the maiden was left in her trance alone,
  To gaze o'er the waves as they danced and played ;
And the waves still danced, and the waves still played,
  Not heeding the sighs of the pensive maid.

And, lo ! as the waters went on in their play,
A nymph arose, and with magic sway
Enchanted the maiden from off the shore
To dwell 'neath the ripples forevermore.
And now, on the banks by the poplar tree,
  Each day, when the sun is aloft on his way,
A nymph may be seen in an ecstasy
  To gaze o'er the waves as they dance and play ;
And the waves still dance, and the waves still play,
And the smiles of the maiden are seen in the spray.

TALAKEENA'S CHASE.

The horns awoke the sleeping dell ;
The notes re-echoed, rose and fell,
    And bounded up again ;
Tree, rock and hill spoke out at once,
Uttering back a quick response,
    And roused the dale and glen.

The beat of hoof, the lash, the shout
Soon put a cowering roe to rout,
    And made his limbs more fleet :
He stood awhile his ears to prick,
Then sprang from out his covert thick,
    And fled with flying feet.

At this another yell arose ;
Three hundred Indians wild did close
    On the pursuing track ;
Again the dells caught up the shout,
Again the rocks and hills spoke out,
    And flung the echoes back.

The roe, with fast upheaving breast,
And with uplifted antlered crest,
      Defied the huntsmen all ;
His nostrils, large expanded wide.
Sniffing the air with lordly pride :
      He scorned the fear of fall.

Now bounded he in winged haste :
Now paused for rest, but to be chased
      And hunted as before ;
Then darted he among the brush,
Where mounted horsemen failed to rush,
      But where their darts could pour.

Again impetuous was he driven,
Nor rest nor hope of rest was given ;
      The merest pause were woe.
But lo ! he's baffled by the brook ;
He turns with bold, defiant look,
      And glares upon his foe.

They whoop and yell, they near and near,
With gleaming eye and thirsty spear,
      Full certain of the beast :
Not so, for, like the feathered wand
From bow-string twanged by mighty hand,
      He darts with lowered crest.

Down drops the chieftain's mustang ; down
The next, a third, a fourth is thrown,
      And tossed in wild dismay ;
Bold Talakeena gains his feet,
But, chid by Alkrane's accents sweet,
      Smites not the noble prey.

The deer with winged fleetness fled ;
Three hundred arrows madly sped
      And passed him like a breath.
Again the streamlet checked his course ;
Again he turned him round perforce,
      This time, to wait for death.

His breath was scant, his strength was low,
Else he again might face his foe,
   And charge them as before.
Three hundred bows were bent full quick
Till both horns met with sudden click :
   Then silence hovered o'er.

But through the still aerial deep,
Like horns when night is fast asleep,
   Rang Talakeena's cry,—
" Forbear, my braves, forbear ! the beast
Has fought his battle well at least ;
   Such foemen should not die."

Awhile the roe remained dismayed,
Awhile he gazed on man and blade,
   Then fled in utter daze.
The warriors marveling glance about,
And up went echoing yell and shout
   In Talakeena's praise.

ALKRANE'S SONG OF LOVE.

IN IMITATION OF MOORE.

O, spirit of rapture, my soul is awake ;
  Give me thoughts that may sparkle like stars in the sky,
Whose beauty is seen in the slumbering lake ;
  Tune my voice to the note of the songsters that fly.
O bright are the moon and the twinkling star
  That climb the mysterious realm above ;
But mine is a theme more charming by far—
  It is love ; it is love.

The sunflowers that bask in the sun's welcome rays,
  The blossoms that bathe in the dew-drops of night,
The realm of the sprites, and the realm of the fays,
  All share of the sweetness of love's delight ;
But theirs is but sadness compared with the bliss
  Of the monarch of hearts in his magical cove ;
O if ever joy smiled for a passion to kiss,
  It is love ; it is love.

The roses of spring-time that blossom and bloom,
  The flowers that laugh in their mute delight,
All live, all perish, all sink in their tomb,
  But love, like a star, shines forever and bright.
The soul that is blest with such magic as this,
  Enchantments are his, which are gifts from above;
For if ever there breathed a spirit of bliss,
  It is love; it is love.

O mine is a theme like the slumbering lake,
Which sleeps till its waves by force borrowed awake:
I drop but a thought, a pebble, and lo!
Ripples on ripples in beauty flow;
And the myriad stars that twinkle and peep
  Are seen in the depths, a beauteous sight,
Flowing and sparkling through the deep,
  As the fires of love in a dream of delight.

Mine is a song whose mystic strain
Awakes a joy in the dullest brain:
I strike but a string and the music rolls,
Spreading a light through the darkest souls;
And mine are the words whose enchanting sway
  Entices the angels of bliss to me:
I need but to whisper, and all obey:
  My hearers rush forth in an ecstasy.

'Tis I that waft to the weary breast
A life-giving hope and a placid rest;
I need but to breathe upon distress
And the heart throbs calm in happiness;
And 'tis I that murmur in sweetest tone
  The secret to pleasures long sought in vain;
Even memory grasps up a joy that is gone,
  And kindles it into life again.

O mine is a song whose gentle truth
Awakens a hope in the hapless youth:
I need but to echo young love's desire,
And his heart is filled with impulsive fire:

Yea, the breast that my bursts of music find
  Bounds and heaves in its wild delight,
As the water, tossed by a pleasant wind,
  Gladdens, exultant in its might.
'Tis I that tell of a coming joy,
And 'tis I that the lingering grief destroy ;
I breathe, and the future is come, and o'er ;
I sing, and the sorrows are no more.
O there are times when hearts descry
  A storm long ere it is thundered forth,
As the birds of the air know the rain is nigh
  Before a drop is seen on the earth.
But what is this wondrous power of mine,
With its mystic music, so pure and fine,
A lay which from dreamland flutters and floats
On the wings of its vague but enchanting notes?
Is it a spell which to fairies belong ?
  Is it a gift from the spirits above ?
Tis both and 'tis more, for the soul of my song
  Is the everywhere monarch, the magic of love.
The flowers of spring-time that blossom and bloom,
  The roses that laugh in their mute delight,
All, live, all perish, all sink in their tomb,
  But love, like a star, shines forever and bright.
The heart that is blest with such magic as this,
  Enchantments are his, which are gifts from above !
O if ever there breathed a spirit of bliss,
  It is love ; it is love !

ALKRANE'S PROPHECY.

  Wake, ye hills that slumber,
    Wake, and tell my spirit ;
  Tell me of the future,
    That I may not fear it;
  That I may proclaim it
    To my fellow creatures,
  To avoid the dangers ;
    Wake, and be my teacher.

Speak, ye darksome forests,
   Speak, and chase the gloominess !
Has our future sunshine?
   May our hopes be luminous?
Speak, ye pine trees, tell me,
   Set your plumed crests humming,
Shall our country conquer
   In the warfare coming ?

Wake, ye lakes—ye placid
   Mighty sleeping waters—
Wake, inspire my spirit,
   Warn your sons and daughters.
Wake, O wake, and warn them :
   Scatter forth your glories,
Pour to them your wisdom,
   I will breathe your stories.

O, ye hills, ye mountains,
   O, ye woods and waters,
Burst from out your slumber,
   Save your sons and daughters.
Sing, and gush forth knowledge,
   One impetuous number,
One wild flood of music ;
   Burst, O burst from slumber.

Ho, my soul arouses,
   All my senses waken :
Nature hears her children—
   We are not forsaken.
Lo ! the valley's beauties
   Rise, and chant before us ;
All their voices mingle
   In tumultuous chorus.
Now, within my fancy
   Images are growing :
Throngs of vaguest spirits
   Flowing, flowing, flowing.

Rising to their brightest :
   Shadows follow after,
After, after, after,
   Robed in sorrow, swelling,
Shaking with grim laughter.
'Tis an omen gloomy,
   'Tis an omen fearful,
One that makes the eyelid
   Droop and quiver tearful.
Lo ! each shape advances,
   Vanishing the brightness :
Where his footstep touches,
   Blackness swallows whiteness.

As the light is victim
   To the shadow shapeless,
Even so is mortal,
   To his fortune hapless.
Light is sniffed by darkness :
   Fate destroys the mortal ;
Both are seized by foemen,
   Swept through dreamland's portal.

O, eternal slumber !
   O, the dream that wakes not !
Sudden sinks the mortal,
   Falls asleep, and wakes not—
Falls asleep, unconscious
   Of the friends that love him—
Heedless of the comrades
   That deplore above him.

Last moon, as I rested,
   Dreaming of the morrow,
Forms assailed my vision,
   Forms of gloom and sorrow ;
And I saw them gliding
   O'er a sweeping river
To the land of spirits,
   There to dwell forever

In canoes of birch-wood,
   Frail canoes, they hurried.
And the storm-blast thundered :
   All seemed lost and buried.
Some gave up the struggle,
   Faint and broken-hearted :
Then, with yells of terror,
   'Neath the waves departed.

Soon do other beings,
   In like birch-wood vessels,
Paddle on together ;
   The storm-blast with them wrestles.
Taking heart and cautious,
   Lest their foe might hurt them,
O'er they rowed triumphant ;
   Faith did not desert them.

Near the shore, a pathway
   Stretched in milky whiteness,
Pathway of the spirits,
   Belt of starry brightness.
This the sprites trod joyful,
   Loving and caressing :
They in faith united,
   Won eternal blessing.

When this vision faded,
   Fast my bosom bounded :
Up I rose affrighted,
   By a gloom surrounded.
" This," moaned I, " is deathful :
   'Tis a woeful omen ! "
Then I wept, and sorrowed,
   Trembling like a woman.

" Woe unto the country ;
   Woe unto the valley,
Whose own sons are faithless,
   Called upon to rally :

Lands whose sons are heartless
    Meet a doom unuttered!"
This, ah, this bewailed I,
    While my sad heart fluttered.

This and more I thought of
    Till my brain, wild glowing,
Whirled and whirled in madness;
    Tree and sky seemed flowing,
Till I sank exhausted,
    Earth my pillow cheerless;
Slumber pressed my eyelids,
    Which not e'en then were tearless.

Long I lay unconscious,
    Mute in blankness sleeping,
With no thrill of feeling
    Through my body creeping.
When I woke all nature
    Hailed me with sweet measures,
Telling wondrous secrets
    Of the future's treasures.

O ye hills, ye mountains,
    O ye woods and waters,
Burst from out your slumber,
    Save your sons and daughters!
Sing, and gush forth courage
    In one thrilling number,
One wild flood of music;
    Burst, O burst from slumber!

ALKRANE'S SONG, MAUKANAW."

O, wild is the heart of the young Maukanaw,
  And wild are the hearts that he leads;
And they live where the bear saps the blood from his paw,
  And they live where the catamount feeds—
In Wyoming's dark mount, where the red flame rests
  Ere it kisses the valley "Good night."

O 'twas there the invaders, with proud-lifted crests,
Came like swallows arrayed against eagle's nests,
  And withered like flowers in a blight ;
Then Maukanaw triumphed, and Maukanaw laughed,
For who could withstand his strong arm and his shaft !

O fierce is the heart of the young Maukanaw,
  And fierce are the hearts of his braves ;
He levels his foes like the Northern flaw,
  Like the leaves you may number their graves.
The tribes of the South and the tribes of the West
  Poured into Wyoming amain ;
And their war-paint was blood-red and blood-red each
    crest,
And wild were the cries round that eagle's nest,
  But they never were heard of again ;
And Maukanaw triumphed, and Maukanaw laughed,
For who could withstand his strong arm and his shaft !

CONFLICT BETWEEN TALAKEENA AND MAUKANAW.

There in the Bison's flowing blood
A towering youth, a chieftain, stood,
  With aspect, wild and gay.
He claimed with mighty utterance,
While brandishing, in pride, his lance,
  That he had slain the prey.

Around him pressed his trusty band
Of warriors with bow in hand,
  Heroes of daring deeds.
They kept their silence, stern and grave,
Till sudden started every brave
  At sounds of coming steeds.

Then flashed their spirits into flame,
And loud and louder rose the name
  Of mighty Maukanaw.

They watched him standing, sullen, dark,
While blazed his eye like meteor spark ;
  A storm-blast there they saw.
Upon the scene the comers swept,
And Talakeena forward stepped,
  And said, " The beast is mine."
But Maukanaw, with brandished blade,
Stood forth, as one for fight arrayed,
  Like some tall plumed pine.

He vowed 'was slain by his own brand,
And, "he that doubts, must face the hand
  By which that prey was won !"
To emphasize his daring phrase,
He flashed his weapon in the rays
  Of the descending sun.

Bold Talakeena bent in scorn,
And plucked the lasso from the horn,
  And from the bleeding head :
Then raised, and held it there on high,
Before the gaze of every eye,
  Streaming with liquid red.

Then casting it away in pride,
He snatched from out the bison's side
  A long and feathered dart,
Which by some sure arm had been sped ;
'Twas bloody red, and brilliant red,
  All colored by the heart.

This, too, he raised and held on high,
Before the gaze of every eye,
  And every brave's comment :
The shaft bore Talakeena's brand,
And feathers, cherished by his band ;
  The truth to all it sent.

Fierce Maukanaw, though now 'twas plain
That beast by him was never slain,
  Yet eager for a fray.

Brandished aloft his flashing spear,
And cried Talakeena, " Here !
   Strike, and win back the prey !' "
Like lightnings through a gathering cloud
Flashed Talakeena's eyes, and loud
   Like thunder rang his call,—
" On with the fight ! here heaves a breast
That fears nor brave nor feathered crest !
   Strike ! thou, or I must fall !' "

Like giants fierce in war arrayed
They rushed together ; blade on blade
   Was shivered wide like grass ;
As when two buffaloes are driven
To strife in fury, horns are riven,
   And scattered o'er the grass.

Awhile the chieftains paused, amazed,
Awhile upon each other gazed,
   Then flashed the hunting knife ;
Again tornado-like they clashed,
Again each blade away was dashed,
   And fiercer grew the strife.

They locked in deadliest embrace,
And war frowned direful in each face :
   Their eyes blazed deathful hopes.
They wrestled like two mountain storms ;
Their sinews stood forth from their forms,
   Like twisted, knotted ropes.

Uprooted grass and stone they hurled,
And round and round they plunged and whirled,
   Breathing like distant thunder :
Then Talakeena strained at length,
His utmost nerve, his utmost strength,
   And crashed his foeman under.

The sound was loud, the echoes lasted :
E'en as a forest oak, when blasted,
   Wakes verberations clear.

Bold Talakeena scowling clasped
His victim's throat, and wildly grasped
  His knife that lay anear.
Fiercely he raised for mightier force,
And poised his blade, and muttered hoarse,
  "Die! daring boaster, die!"
"Smite!" cried the conquered warrior, "smite!
I fear nor brave, nor chief, nor sprite!
  For Maukanaw am I!"

His voice rang like a hunter's horn;
His smile was fierce with pride and scorn;
  Defiant blazed his eye.
Awhile the weapon threatened death;
Awhile it gleamed, then, like a breath,
  Away 'twas seen to fly.
Then Talakeena upward sprung,
While thunder-like his accents rung:
  "Arise, most fearless brave!
'Twere base for hand of warrior
To cause such blood as thine to pour,
  And that, so near yon wave,

The wave that lately blood-red saw
Invaders crushed by Maukanaw,
  Like reeds before a blast.
Here where our fathers bled of old,
Sons of Wyoming, tried and bold!
  O be this strife our last!

"As for the bison, if 'tis mine,
I claim it not, great chief, 'tis thine!
  Thou art Wyoming born!"
Then loud in Talakeena's name
Did deafening yell its praise proclaim,
  And shriek of battle-horn.

The tumult ceased; all silent gazed;
Young Maukanaw abashed, amazed,
  Stood there as in a trance.

Finding his voice at last, he said,
"Met I that mighty chieftain's blade,
  Wyoming's boldest lance?

"Though I have urged to selfish war
Wyoming's noblest warrior,
  I now will make amends!"
Both chieftains smiled, and face to face
They stood, the mightiest of their race,
  Clasping their hands as friends.

TALAKEENA'S BISON CHASE.

Dark rolled the dust-cloud o'er the plain;
A herd of bisons dashed amain,
  Impetuous in their flight.
The Indians, all with bridle slack,
Fast followed on the bisons' track,
  Yelling in high delight.

The herd plunged fierce and fiercer still,
And swept along the rocky hill,
  Wild prancing as they went.
The bold Wyoming kept the rear,
Yet up rang hopeful shout and cheer
  And laugh of merriment.

The noble chief his lasso drew,
And with a whirling motion threw,
  Circling a bison's neck.
His comrades, at the signal word,
Grappled upon the tightened cord,
  The victim's speed to check.

Then rose again a boisterous roar,
More wild, more deafening than before,
  And more discordant tones.
The beast, to madness driven, at length
Jumped and tossed with mightier strength,
  Uprooting grass and stones.

At last the lasso snapped like thread ;
The bison sprang, and off he sped,
   Exulting in his might ;
But, as around the hill he dashed,
Bold Talakeena's arrow flashed,
   And deadly was its flight.

TALAKEENA AT EVENING.

A FRAGMENT.

O'er Campbell's Ledge the sun had flown,
And now was slowly gliding down
Behind the western mountain's crown.

Bold Talakeena saw the rays
   Glance wild into the valley ;
Brief on the ledge then did he gaze,
The Red-man's clock which shone ablaze,
   Then bade his braves to rally.

And at the word the trusty band,
With lash and bridle rein in hand,
   Sped off athwart the plain ;
And though the day had wearied all,
Their spirits never seemed to fall ;
   They whooped and yelled again.

And soon, from out the wood near by,
There fled a doe, and every eye
   Lit up with zest ;
Three hundred lashes cut the air,
Three hundred voices struck despair
   Into the fleeing beast.

Though fleet the steed of every brave
To scale the crag, to stem the wave,
   To speed in level race,
Bold Talakeena's mustang burst
Forth from the throng, triumphant, first,
   And led the flying chase.

TALAKEENA'S BATTLE WITH THE WHITE MEN.

'Twas eve, and the sun, all aglow in the west,
Behind the wild mountain was sinking to rest ;
O'er the high peaks it lingered ere taking its flight,
As if 'twere reluctant to leave such a sight.
It lit all the valley with beauty, and spread
Its smiles o'er the river which sang as it sped
With laugh and with ripple of music along ;
And sweet was its laughter, and sweet was its song.

The valley lay smiling in Solitude's arms,
And Nature, though falling to sleep, gave her charms.
The air hovered motionless over the glen,
With naught to disturb it, except, now and then,
When the hoot of an owl could be faintly heard,
Or the far-away chirp of an evening bird,
Or the sigh or the voice of a whispering breeze,
Breathing its fairy-like melodies.

Thus Nature dreamed on in her peaceful repose ;
But suddenly up from the river there rose
A sound like the splashing of oars on the stream,
And the valley, awaking, broke forth from her dream—
Forever broke forth, for soon boat after boat
Appeared on the wave like an army afloat ;
Nearer and nearer they drew to the land,
And, lo ! a small fleet struck at last on the sand.

Their flags are unfurled, and their banners are spread,
With their crimson and gold and their brilliant red :
And beneath the clear sun waxes brighter their sheen,
As triumphant they dance o'er the beauteous scene.
The white man, the white man, he comes to explore
The old Susquehanna, and settle her shore ;
To plunder the slumbering Wyoming vale,
To steal her fair beauty from upland and dale.

First hurried the women and children astrand,
Then followed the men, a warlike band,
Fully equipped with musket and lance
To fight their way through the wild expanse.
They drew up their boats on the river's green side,
For safety there from the dash of the tide.
No word was spoken, or syllable e'en ;
No jocund laugh broke the pure serene :
Nor a smile nor a frown could be seen on a face
To mar the soft influence of the place ;
But they stood as entranced in a wondering gaze,
And mutely poured forth to the scenery their praise.

But lo ! the loud trample of horses was heard !
And over a hillock, all dabbled and blurred
With blood from her wounds, sped a deer in alarm ;
She shot past the whites without scathe, without harm.
Her nostrils were spouting out blood through the air,
Her large eyes were bloodshot, and wore a wild glare,
And within those orbs, all dilated and bleeding,
There shone a light so pathetic and pleading,
Which touched and melted all gazes it met,
And all that beheld it could never forget.

On, on sped the doe in her perilous track,
Flashing her terrified glances back ;
And behind dashed the Reds at a furious pace,
And bold Talakeena was first in the chase.

But when he beheld the intruders so near,
He ceased his pursuit of the poor panting deer,
And, sitting erect on his foaming steed,
He drew on his bridle and slackened his speed ;
Then wheeling about to his comrades, he said :—
" Behold ye yon stranger, nor quail ye, nor dread?
O warriors, O friends ! who here would be braves ?
Who here would be cowards ? who here would be slaves ?
If such a man breathe here, quick let him withdraw !
Let him serpent-like slink ! let him live as a squaw !

If freedom ye love, O my warriors true,
That freedom this hour must be purchased by you !
You pale-face invaders, though many they stand,
At once we must scatter and drive from our land ;
For our vale and for Manito charge at my cry,
And ere the sun sinks we will conquer or die ! ''

Lo ! sudden he uttered a war-whoop so shrill,
That echoed and re-echoed over the hill ;
Then down like a whirlwind of fury they came,
And soon were enveloped in smoke and in flame.
They sent up their hoot, and their curse, and their yell ;
They plunged like fierce demons late loosed out of hell.

The white men stood still as the motionless air,
Some ranged in a line, some ranged in a square ;
Calmly the charge of the Indians they stayed,
Calmly they checked it with shot and with blade.
They stood like a rock, till their foemen drew near,
Then smote and o'erwhelmed them with musket and spear ;
Their knowledge, their discipline, weapon and shield,
Made them the victors, the lords of the field.

The Red-men fell back, but again did they try :
They mustered to charge, they charged but to die.
Twice in succession they led the attack,
Twice were they driven demoralized back,
Leaving all mangled the most of their men,
Whose riderless chargers dashed off through the glen.
They mustered their forces once more, and still brave,
For one final charge to their '' glory or grave ;''
For a moment their devilish tumult seemed quelled,
For a moment again, and they cursed and they yelled ;
Then onward, then onward, they swept and were led
By bold Talakeena, who galloped ahead.

They routed the square that the white men had formed,
And, darting within it, they battled and stormed,
And slaughtered, with terror on every hand,
Nigh blasting to ruin the mighty white band.

Near, near was their goal ! near, near their success !
And bright was the glory their valor might bless.
Alas, for the white men ! alas, for their skill !
They scattered, they fled, and they mounted the hill :
They strove to its summit, there silent they stood,
And awaited a charge from the men of the wood.

The Red-men, now frenzied with hatred and pride,
Impetuous, clambered the hill's rugged side ;
Lo ! sudden a yell of dismay wildly rang,
While bristled the arms with their clatter and clang,
For down rushed the whites at a furious run,
Spreading a havoc with sabre and gun,
Smiting like giants, and, careless of life,
Shooting and mowing their way through the strife ;
And as thundered they forth their explosion and stroke,
The field became veiled in a curling smoke,
And the sharp cry of pain and agony's yell
Told that full many an Indian fell ;
They dropped by dozens, they writhed in gore,
Tearing the grass, to breathe no more.
Their comrades stood, whooped, then away they fled,
Some falling in death on their mangled dead,
Some seeking the wood in their utter despair,
Sending their shrieks through the dismal air ;
And all that escaped stole away to the heights,
And left the red field in the hands of the whites.

The wild and fierce battle was over and won ;
And lo ! on the hillside, unhorsed and alone,
Undaunted, unscathed, a tall Indian stood,
His long knife still dripped with his enemies' blood :
His hair floated wildly about on the air,
As if in defiance, as if in despair ;
No shadow of fear nor of shame marred his face ;
He looked on defeat without thought of disgrace.
But his haughty lip curled with a bitter scorn ;
He seemed the noblest chieftain born.

His proud breast was heaving, and fast came his breath,
He stood, like a warrior, waiting his death.
The white men approached him, he threw down his knife
And folded his arms to surrender his life.
Then, placing his hand on his bosom, he said :
"Strike here, coward pale-face, yea, I'm not afraid
To lie with my comrades in death and in gore,
To chase the wild deer and the bison no more.
You have ruined my tribe, my valley, my all !
Now strike at my heart ! I am ready to fall !"
The leader then turned to his comrades and said :—
"The courage and conduct of this noble red
Are worthy of praise to the highest degree,
And we shall most certainly let him go free."
He said to the chieftain, "Go, go where you will !"
And bold Talakeena descended the hill.
Yet undaunted his heart, and unconquered his pride,
'Twas for vengeance he strode toward the wild mountain-
    side.

NONSENSE AND NOISE.

O say what you may against nonsense and noise,
    But give a good proof for your saying ;
For my part, the children, the girls and the boys,
    Distract the worst care with their playing.

And what were this life if a noise, now and then,
    Or a nonsense should not break the quiet?
Such oft has been sweetmeat to wisest of men,
    When oppressed by their heavier diet.

Alas for the big boy, the half-learned man,
    The old maid, and the young high-school lady !
For endure children's tumult those souls never can ;
    Thus their dignity waxes more shady.

Then here's to the children, the girls and the boys ;
    I will join with their laughing and playing ;
And say what you may against nonsense and noise,
    But give a good proof for your saying.

WEEP NOT.

IN MEMORY OF MR. W. C.

Weep not, weep not for the fond, fond one
Whose toils are o'er and whose race is run !
For happier far is that lasting sleep
Than all the joys that life's treasures keep.
Weep not, weep not for our absent friend ;
    Weep not, weep not for his early doom,
But let the dews from the heavens descend,
    And like tears from the angels, besprinkle his tomb.

Let music flow soft, and let roses be strown,
As a token of love to the soul that is flown ;
Nor weep, nor mourn, but murmur a prayer
That shall echo in heaven, and gladden him there.
O his are the sighs that delight's bosom heaves !
    O his is a soul that shall sorrow no more !
But alas ! ah, alas ! for the widow that grieves !
    The lorn, lorn heart that is left to deplore.

Could the angels have looked from their sphere above
And gazed on his acts of sweet duty and love,
They joyous would sing in that realm of bliss,
And receive to their choir a good spirit from this.
Weep not, weep not for the soul that is fled ;
    Weep not for the friend that shall greet us no more,
But sigh for the lorn heart that grieves o'er her dead,
    The sad, sad heart that is left to deplore.

THE PIG AND THE DRUNKARD.

One day in a mud-hole there wallowed a pig,
    With his brother, the drunkard beside him ;
And a preacher, while passing, gave each a hard dig,
    And coolly remarked, as he eyed him,—
"'This maxim of old will forever hold good,
    ' By his company one may be known : '"
Then straightway the pig fled as fast as he could,
    With a certain respect of his own.

RECOLLECTIONS OF SCHOOL DAYS.

TO F. M.

O there are bards who've waked the string
A lay of cupid's own to sing,
And though the harp hath oft unstrung
Long ere the theme was fully sung,
Yet whether broke or whether loose
The lay went, aided by the muse,
Far, far o'er rapture's height ascending,
And at a lofty climax ending.

If love-lay to great bards be such
That wakes ecstatic by the touch,
And e'en when reft of music's wings,
Still onward soars, still onward sings,
Then from a harp like mine one sound
Of worth, at least, must needs resound.

If such be true, then muse to me,
And aid me in my minstrelsy ;
For next to Cupid's is my theme—
'Tis friendship, of my youth a dream.

O Frank, my friend, 'tis sweet to think
     Of times, of school-days that are o'er,
When memories, with their magic link
     Joys unto joys that are no more.

'Tis sweet to contemplate the hours
When boyhood plucked life's thornless flowers,
     And held them in his grasp ;
But sweeter far it is to me
To meet once more, and fervently,
     A schoolmate's eager clasp.

I dreamed a wakeful dream last night,
     A dream that I have often dreamed :
Again I drank of youth's delight—
     What an elysium it seemed.

While wandering in this joyous trance,
    Back to the old school I returned,
And there I met full many a glance
    And many a soul that wanton burned,
And many a heart and many a hand
    That I had often met before :
The school-boys in a laughing band
    Greeted me at the open door.

And there amidst the merry throng
Came Malcolm, frolicking along—
Malcolm, the merriest of the group,
With his ringing laugh and his ringing whoop—
Malcolm, the buxom, blithesome boy,
Whose very self was a bubbling joy.

O blest the hour ! O blest the minute
    When school-boy clasps a school-boy friend !
What fleetness then the day has in it !
    It comes, 'tis here, 'tis at an end.

Mere friendship's voice and touch may dart
A pleasure through the dullest heart,
    A pleasure, sweet, exquisite :
But sweeter, more exquisite still,
The trembling joy, the magic thrill,
To hear the voice, to feel the touch
Of friends by us beloved so much—
    A nameless transport is it.

Thus happy interchanged we greetings,
    I and that laughing school-boy band :
Yet still, O still I craved more meetings
    Of throbbing heart and thrilling hand.

Slowly the bevy turned away :
Hither and thither scattered they,
Some to their books, and some to play,
While up went shout and wild halloo,
And merry peals of laughter, too :
Thus did they romp and wanton on,
And, sighing, I thought myself alone.

A laugh of music charmed my ear ;
I turned, and Malcolm still was near.
His voice in wild endearment rung,
And to the accents sweet I clung ;
And I blest that heart, and I blest that tongue.

Smiling a sweetly happy smile,
I grasped his hand, and said the while,
" Laugh on, laugh on, while laugh you may,
    My boy, with heart so full of glee ;
And may such friendship hold its sway
    For aye within that bosom free.
Laugh on, laugh on in all your joy !
Be e'er a merry laughing boy. "

Then, arm in arm, slow strayed we o'er
    The shady gravel walk,
As we had often strayed before,
    With many a friendly talk.
And sad, yet strangely sweet it seemed,
    As thoughtfully we trod,
To think that there my boyhood dreamed,
    And pressed the self-same sod.

But lo ! there soon appeared a lad
    With pale and thoughtful face ;
Yet a cheerful tone his clear voice had,
    And his hand a warm embrace ;
Still wore he that pale thoughtful look,
As if he meant to write a book,
    And wonders in it trace.

" Ellis," sighed I, " Ellis, dear,"
    Holding his hand in mine,
" Thou wert e'er here, thou still art here,
    Haunting this haunt of thine.

" How oft have we together strayed
    To spend the evening in thought ;
How oft at noontide 'neath the shade
    Into the depths of lore we've sought ;

How often, O how often still
Have we delighted——" here a thrill
  Of joy my spirit overwrought.

Then stood we still, no word was spoke,
But Ellis fond the silence broke ;
His joyful heart bade words to speed,
And they were hearty words indeed.

Then smiled we, and then moved on,
Conversing in a happy tone ;
Still craved my heart for something yet—
One friend remained I had not met.

Just then a violin was heard,
Now, like the warbling of a bird,
Now, like a brook between the hills,
And now, like distant mountain rills,
And then, like an angel did it seem,
And then like a demon in his dream.

One moment stood I overjoyed,
  One moment stood I in a trance,
One more the spell was all destroyed,
  The air my voice cut like a lance.

"O, Fra Diavalo!" I cried,
  "O, Fra Diavalo!"
The music ceases, footsteps glide,
  And Frank is here below.

O, Frank ! but think what joy was ours,
  As, straying arm in arm,
We talked of by-gone happy hours,
When culled we boyhood's choicest flowers,
  And revelled in their charm.

When turned we all we knew to fun,
  Turned we to sport our gravest lore ;
Then sighed we at our knowledge spun,
  And sighed we that we knew no more.

O what a pleasure memory gives
   When memory's real actors meet ;
The dim past in the present lives,
   And every act is good and sweet.

Thus roamed we on, how brief did seem
   The moments as they glided ;
But soon, too soon dissolved my dream,
   My storm of joy subsided.

Then sad and sadder grew my soul,
While veiling gloom'ness round me stole ;
For, friend, these words are from his lips
Who keen the sweets of friendship sips,
Who even in heaven should despair
Could friends of his not meet him there.

Nor scorn the bosom fond that burns
And for another bosom yearns.
The tender heart, like tender vine,
Round something near it needs must twine ;
And separate them if you will,
They'll keep their former semblance still.

Alas, alas ! for breasts that feel
No thrill of friendship through them steal !
Alas, alas ! too, for the heart
That never throbs to Cupid's dart !
For love and friendship nobly given
Are blessings from the throne of heaven ;
Friendship and love, twin sanctities,
O what could heaven give more than these ?

But Frank, morn smiles ! the moments fly,
And I must off to industry.
The hours of toil each other chase,
And I must enter in the race
To sow and reap what good I can ;
Such is the duty of a man.

Farewell, these lips that failed to tell
Even half the warmth, the glow, I feel,
Even half the worth of friendship's weal,
Now tremble forth a fond farewell.

MY SOUL.

As the sunshine feeds the flower
  And smiles it into beauty,
So did childhood's fire empower
  My soul with love and duty.

As the mountain oak is marred,
  All knotted by the storm,
So my soul by sin is scarred
  And twisted out of form.

TO MY SISTER MAY,

ON HER FOURTEENTH BIRTHDAY.

Again the Christmas bells awake,
Again their flight the echoes take
From every turret, tower and steeple,
Flinging a gladness to the people,
Whose hearts, while listening to the chime,
Have voices in them keeping time—
Voices that speak, and speak again
Of " Peace on earth, good will to men ! "

Again the hills are white with snow,
And wild as fourteen years ago,
When, as a blessing from above,
A Christmas gift of joy and love
Entered our household, and with smile
And laugh 'gan straightway to beguile
Our hearts from care, the hours to speed,
And I a sister had, indeed.

The seasons fierce have o'er thee blown,
And still thy smiles are brighter grown;
But the same fourteen winters dark
That breathed on thee and fanned the spark
Of life which glowed in thy slight frame,
Kindling it into ardent flame,
On my breast blew an icy breath,
And quenched the fire that burned beneath.

I hoped as you now hope, but fast
Withered each hope before the blast
Of pitiless adversity.
Friends of my heart were torn from me—
You knew Glycæa, ever true
Playmate of yours and mine, but you,
Merely an infant, could not know
What ardor made her bosom glow.

Then O how lovely Anna bloomed!
How her sweet smile and glance illumed
With joy the face on which they shone!
But both, alas, are faded—flown!
Glycæa 'neath yon snow-drift sleeps,
There where the lonely willow weeps;
And Anna hath her cold, cold grave
By Lackawanna's wild-voiced wave.

Such grief it was, and more, far more
Than e'er was dreamt, that gnawed the core
Of my seared heart with pangs untold,
And made me as I am, so old,
And rent the chasm that intervenes
Our ages—both are in our teens;
I end them, thou dost but begin;
Thine is pure youth, and mine gray sin.

Time was when sunny smiles were mine,
Sunny and good, my May, as thine;
When I, with blithesome heart and gay,
Could laugh another's gloom away,

Free as the butterfly I chased,
And just as wild ; my mind embraced
Things joyful, and dispelled the sad ;
And every day brought something glad.

But now, what am I ?   The mere wreck
Of sweet hours, when nor rein could check,
Nor hand could tame, nor tongue reprove,
Joy's slave, and votary of love.
Yet, why thus idly prate ?   You know
The story of my weal and woe !
Far better 'twere for me to state
How you might shun a brother's fate.

Live in the present and, with care,
Blessings for future days prepare,
Nor let thy mind take idle wings,
To dally over by-gone things,
Letting the living moments fly—
The golden moments—ah, 'tis I
That have the right to give advice !
And let, ay, let my word suffice !

But for thy prototype in life
O take not me ; my long-lived strife
Hath been a retrospection mere,
A backward gaze, a sigh, a tear ;
For mine hath ever been to moan
The times and pleasures that are flown,
The friends whose lots with mine were cast ;
My heart, my being is in the past.

E'en when a boy how oft I strayed
Off from my comrades, as they played,
And sought remote sequestered bowers,
There to regret my childhood hours ;
And when a child, at eventide,
How for the morning's fun I sighed ;
How, when awake at break of day,
I wept the joys of yesterday.

All this was weakness, and the fruit
Was thorns; the fault thou may'st impute
To wanton will; such habits shun.
By present action most is won;
Thy heart to goodly deeds atune;
Goodness can not be used too soon,
For fast, ah, fast a life is run,
It ends before 'tis well begun.

But this is Christmas day, and I
Do naught but preach, complain and sigh,
When joy, enthroned within my heart,
Its thrill to others should impart.
Come, I will smile and sing to-day,
And join the children in their play,
Whilst thou, whose tones disperse the sadness,
Wilt laugh my Christmas into gladness.

ENTOMBED COAL MINERS AT SOUTH WILKESBARRE.

A SONG, WRITTEN BY THE REQUEST OF J. M. ESQ.

O why do the women and children despair
    As they gather on yonder fair slope?
Can it be that grim death is a reveler there—
    The blaster of many a hope?
How they weep, as they stare at the shaft below,
    Where the creaking ropes deepen the gloom,
And the black tower frowns like a spectre foe!
Ah, the poor bereaved bosoms groan loud in their woe!
    For their dear ones are deep in that tomb.

CHORUS:

They despair, they despair! and the teardrops fall fast,
    But they weep and they sorrow in vain;
For their loved ones are cast like the leaves in the blast,
    And they never shall meet them again.

That woman, all frantic, why laughs she so wild?
  Her husband, alas, is no more !
And mad now she sings to her innocent child ;
  Ay, she laughs while her neighbors deplore.
And there sorrows a mother, distracted and lorn,
  And a father with grief is o'ercome ;
They grieve for a son who, at early morn,
With a smile waved his hand, then away was torn,
  Forever, forever from home.

Cho.—They despair, they despair ! etc.

O the cold-hearted lords of black diamond hills !
  Though they hold the poor miner a slave,
How little they guard against dangers and ills,
  Ere the mine is turned into a grave !
Even now how little they care for the tears
  Of the widows who wail in their woe !
And the moans of fond parents fall not on their ears !
But unheeded those mourners o'er tenantless biers
  Hand in hand with lank poverty go.

Cho.—They despair, they despair ! etc.

EVENING IN SUMMER.

The sun, with outstretched golden wing,
    Descends with splendor fierce ; and now
    He fades on the horizon's brow,
  With all the grandeur following.
The sweet-voiced birds no longer sing ;
    But owls and tree-toads from the bough
    Pour forth their dismal sounds below,
  Whence echoes, just as dismal, ring.
Now deep and deeper grows the shade
    On twilight's robes of purple haze,
    Which thicken silently, and fall
  With awe that makes me half afraid,
  And prompts my soul to utter praise
    To him that watcheth over all.

CALEPSYCHE.

"O Calepsyche!   Calepsyche!"
  This I uttered,
My wild heart bleeding, aching,
  As it fluttered, fluttered, fluttered,
When, from sleep awaking,
  Up I started,
In time to know my heart was breaking:
  In dreamland we had parted!
Calepsyche!   Calepsyche!
O my lost, lost Calepsyche!
  Thy face beamed forth celestial whiteness;
  All thy form was starry brightness,
  Thou hast left my heart all blightness,
Calepsyche!
Beauteous, radiant Calepsyche
"O Calepsyche!   "Calepsyche!"
  This I uttered when awaking,
  As I felt my heart-strings breaking.
In dreamland we had met and parted,
She the pure, the simple hearted;
O, the bliss her lips imparted!
The goodness which her glances darted!
  She spake her name; that name I caught not!
  But the sound my soul forgot not;
  Such sweet music Orpheus taught not.
  Her magic name I knew not, sought not,
But I named her Calepsyche!
Calepsyche!   Calepsyche!
O, my wondrous Carepsyche,
  With beauty as fair as the sunlit air!
Hast thou dissolved to a thought of sweetness?
  O, dream of a breath, whose flight gives me death!
Why hast thou blasted my heart by thy fleetness?
  Yet high by the throne of heaven,
  When bliss to me is given,
I shall behold my Calepsyche!
Beauteous, radiant Calepsyche!

GOOD-BYE, MY FRIEND.

TO CLEMATIS.

Good-bye my friend, a short good-bye !
   And though I sigh in pain,
I'd bid thy bosom not to sigh ;
   We soon shall meet again.

We soon shall meet—O hopeful thought,
   Thou cheat'st a bitter sorrow !
For if this hope thou had'st not brought,
   I scarce could brook the morrow.
But we shall meet, my loving boy,
   So dash those tears away ;
My breast is pained when ought but joy
   Thy big warm drops obey.

Come, I will kiss thy burning cheek,
   And then thine eye may dry.
Now, let thy voice of music speak ;
   We'll sigh a fond good-bye.

Good-bye, my friend, a short good-bye !
   My memory sweet retain ;
Nor sigh nor weep, for thou and I
   Shall meet, O soon again.

LINES FOR AN AUTOGRAPH ALBUM.

O, as you read these lines, my dear,
   When years have glided by,
Still think of him that wrote them here,
   Still breathe for him a sigh.

FOR THE SAME.

What ! write my name upon this page ?
   Thou hast o'erwhelmed me quite,
Not that thy charms do not engage,
   No, no, but I can't write !

TO MISS M.

WHO, AT OUR FIRST MEETING, REQUESTED ME TO ADDRESS HER A POEM.

O many a minstrel hath been swayed
To ecstacy by lovely maid,
   To whose fond word and fond desire
   He breathed his soul's intensest fire :
But they, ah, they sent looks that stole
A secret thrill from soul to soul—
   A thrill called love, whose mystic art
   Let each into the other's heart.

Such, such has been, and such shall be,
So long as love is poesy :
   But, ah, my fair one, how, I pray,
   Can thy fond wish hold magic sway
O'er my dull soul, or e'en give birth
To thoughts that waft a sweetness forth,
   When thus to thee my heart's unknown,
   And I am stranger to thy own ?

Had e'er our souls each other showed,
Had e'er our breaths commingling glowed,
And had thy blushing face, the while,
Broke into dimples with thy smile,
And had thy voice, thy sigh, thy kiss,
Added their music to my bliss,
O then could all my rapture spring !
Then, then could I thy praises sing !

But no ; 'tis idle thus to run,
With wanton tongue, in song to one
Whose touch is strange, whose voice is strange :
Yet voice and touch, in time, may change !
However, here's a fond farewell :
And though we're strangers, I might tell
I've caught one joy to bliss akin,
A glimpse of thy sweet self within.

AN ANSWER.

ON BEING ASKED WHY SO MANY VERSES WERE
ADDRESSED TO CLEMATIS.

What! ask me, dunce, why more than once
   I've sung to young Clematis?
My songs read'st thou. Thy question, now,
   But shows how dull thy pate is.

TO PHOEBE.

O Phoebe, thine was cruel wrong,
Hinting that I should take to song!
For fatal, fatal proved thy hints—
I have been singing ever since!

GLYCÆA.

O fled is Glycæa, too tender for grief,
   And too good for the world we have here;
She withered away like a frost-bitten leaf,
And her spirit is gone, 'tis my happy belief,
   To inhabit some heavenlier sphere.

How the hearts the beloved of her bosom unite,
   At times, and commingle their tears,
And sorrow for one who robbed gloom from the night,
Who smiled, and the cloudiest day appeared bright,
   And whose voice was a balm to the ears.

No more, ah, no more will her beauty endear!
   No more will her smile chase the gloom!
And never again will her voice charm the ear;
And never again will she calm our worst fear,
   For they've hid her away in the tomb.

O they've hid her away in the willow tree's shade,
   Where the mosses are burdened with snow;
And I know she'd complain of the grave where she's laid,
For 'tis lonely and cold, ah, too cold for a maid,
   Whose heart like Glycæa's could glow.

TO CALLIE.

There are times when a note to the bosom may dart,
   Where, in after years, yet it can thrill ;
Even so may this wish wing its way to thy heart,--
   When I'm absent, O think of me still.

TO CLEMATIS.

Clematis when we sighed farewell,
   I thought 'twas for a fortnight only ;
Hope of soon meeting gave the spell
   Which kept my heart from growing lonely.

But now that hope has turned to fear,
   That spell has ceased its charmed endeavor,
And in my throbbing heart I hear
   The knell that we shall meet, ah, never !

Weep not, dear boy, I don't impart
   These words to set thy bosom aching ;
They're but the echos of my heart,
   And it but moans because 'tis breaking.

Yet why thus moan ?　Have I no hope ?
   A dim spark gleams, but half averted,
Which with my gloominess cannot cope,
   But makes me feel the more deserted.

O ! if our hands should never meet,—
   Ah, now my pangs find vent in weeping !
This boon I ask: that memory sweet
   Of me may keep thy love from sleeping.

But as for me, Clematis mine,
   My love for thee can ne'er be clouded ;
Ere thoughts of thee can cease to shine,
   My mem'ry's self must be enshrouded.

ON THE BANKS OF SUSQUEHANNA.

TO THE TUNE OF "ALLEN WATER."

On the banks of Susquehanna,
  'Mid Wyoming's fairest bowers,
Smiled and bloomed my lovely Anna,
  Sister of the flowers.
Like the laugh of Lackawanna
  Was her voice to sing or speak ;
Like the smiles on Susquehanna
  Dimpled bright her cheek.

On the banks of Susquehanna,
  As the day began to fade,
O how blest was I with Anna !
  How enrapt we strayed !
From my bower to Lackawanna
  By no rose was she out-bloomed ;
By the sheen on Susquehanna
  Was her youth illumed.

On the banks of Susquehanna
  Winged a fever's withering flight ;
Then, ah, then was lost my Anna—
  Day to me was night !
Now I haunt wild Lackawanna,
  Where her voice the ripples give ;
Still I stray by Susquehanna—
  There her bright smiles live.

TRUE HAPPINESS.

Be happy, be happy, I bid the sad mind,
  But learn what true happiness is :
When a dutiful man has a heart good and kind,
  True happiness surely is his.

MY REPENTANCE.

Ah, once I tried some wit to spin !
    It weighs on me like tons, sir ;
O 'twas an error worse than sin,
    A rhyme bedecked with puns, sir.

But once I've punned, and only once ;
    No more that sin shall shame me ;
Such sickly wit befits the dunce—
    And dunce was I ; don't blame me.

Yea, that's a solace to my pain,
    But once my puns have hurt me :
And if I ever pun again,
    Lord, may the muse desert me.

I'M GROWING OLD.

I'm growing old, I'm growing old,
    Yet scarce my youth is fled ;
The heart which burned so wild is cold,
    The fire within is dead.
There was a time when this weak frame
    Knew love's intensest glow,
And fondest chords caught up the flame,
    And fondest thoughts would flow.

I'm growing old, I'm growing old,
    My soul is ribbed with sin ;
And no one knows how dark and cold
    My bosom is within.
They say my hair is just as black,
    And just as smooth my brow,
But, ah ! they know not what a wrack
    Lies prostrate in me now.

I'm growing old, I'm growing old,
    Though few have been my years,
But many they've seemed, and long and cold,
    I've traced them with my tears.

Yet friends will say I'm young and hale,
　I'm but a boy to-day ;
Ah, could they hear my life's long tale,
　They'd know my age is gray.

I'm growing old, I'm growing old,
　My early friends are flown :
Of all that happy race, I'm told
　That I remain alone.
My life, alas, is off its course !
　Its music out of tune,
Its glowing spring consumed my force,
　Its autumn came in June.

I'm growing old, I'm growing old,
　Yet why my fate deplore ?
Rolls not the world as e'er it rolled ?
　Why mourn the days of yore ?
'Tis I, and not the world, that's wrong ;
　Man make's his rain or shine ;
Then O let duty be my song !
　And happiness is mine.

EPISTLE TO F. M.

A RHAPSODY.

(F. M., nick-named "Fra Diavolo," a musician, who, taking a sudden turn of
mind, began preparations for college.)

Carol, O muse, and aid the flow
Of song to Fra Diavolo ;
And thou, my Fra, prick well thine ear,
For sense and nonsense scribbled here.
Fear not these lines, though some might dread them,
Yet thee I'd warn ere thou hast read them,
" If thou hast tears, prepare to shed them,"
For never since primeval age,
Has such a doggerel blurred a page.
Full curious am I to know
How now thy precious moments go.

How is thy present situation?
What is thy present occupation?
Is thine glad joy, or sad damnation,
Writing some wild instrumentation,
Or trying to memorize, *verbatim*,
Amo, '*are*, '*avi*, '*atum?*

Art thou in arms against the Greek,
While brain grows hot, and courage weak,
Trying to find the reason why
Phero turns into *oisomai?*

Methinks I see—Ha! ha! but O,
Forgive, I pray, this sudden flow
Of merriment—I seem to see—
   Ha! ha! I run, but fun runs after,
And though the fiends should kidnap me,
   I could not now restrain my laughter.

Be calm, my soul, and sit thou still,
Show thy good breeding and good will,
Nor laugh, nor squeak like one insane,
But let me once begin again.

O Frank, I see you as you go,
Pacing the pavement to and fro,
With stiff and measured tread, as one
That wears gay clothes and bears a gun;
Ay, and a dangerous look you show,
Forward and backward, as you go,
With footsteps by the bricks betinkled,
With hair erect, and forehead wrinkled,
With face all pale and dank and sprinkled,
With mind in critical condition,
Wrestling by main strength and ambition
Some geometric proposition.

Lo! suddenly there's heard a cry,
   " Come to the parlor, friends are here!"
The answer is a saw-mill sigh
   And, martyr-like, Frank meets his bier,

Which, by the way, is not eternal,
But called a bier because infernal.

A stool it is, a three-legged stool,
Which, ah, too oft supports a fool.
Now high upon the top you spring,
   And perch you there, no fool, I trow,
No fool ; but O, you seem a thing
   So close resembling one, I vow ;
My neck and ears give forth a smile,
For I've been there and cussed, the while.

And now you set the music going,
And melodies come flowing, flowing,
With wild fantastic variation,
And subtle, intricate imitation.
" What, a sonata is it, folks ? "
He spake, and see, the villain pokes
A neighboring maid with loving dig ;
She answers wisely, " That's a jig ! "

Yet still the player rattles away,
And still the people simper and say,
And the player groans and waxes hot ;
O he could murder on the spot !

But soon the final echoes die,
And round and round the room there fly
Manifold sounds of iron-bound praises,
The same old phrases, same old phrases—
" That's pretty good, that's pretty good !
Remembered it all ! I never could ! "

Meanwhile poor Frank sits like a goose,
Trying to cube the hypothenuse ;
Then some one asks him for a song ;
His proposition comes out wrong.
His throat now gurgles like a frog's,
And away goes Euclid to the dogs.

With deep emotion and strength divine
He sings of love, and he sings it fine—
His favorite—" Ehrin on the Rhine."
But lo ! he talks of soldier's pensions,
And slips, at last, into Latin declensions,
While higher and higher grows his vexation,
Till he ends by beginning a conjugation.
The piano stops, but his voice, how flat !
As he shouts " *amo, amas, amat !* "
Then, springing up in frog-like terror,
He hastes to expiate his error :
Croaks he : "O pardon my mixed knowledge,
I am a candidate for college !' "

AN EARNEST THANKSGIVING ; OR THE DRUNKARD AND HIS BOY.

WRITTEN FOR THE CHILDREN'S THANKSGIVING ENTER-
TAINMENT.

How the little old cottage re-echoes
    With the voices of children at play !
You might know 'tis the Thanksgiving dinner
    That makes them so happy to-day.

There it sits, on the table, the turkey,
    Pumpkin-pie and pudding, and cake ;
And the children but wait for the signal,
    When O, what a havoc they'll make !

The mother, a woman still youthful,
    Though her hair has long been like the snow,
Is more anxious to-day than ever
    To have every item just so.

" Mamma," said bright little Mabel,
    " Never before had we flowers
On the table at Thanksgiving dinner !
    And those napkins, and spoons—are they ours?"

" Hush, child, it is all for your father ;
　　I want to make this one day glad :
For twenty years, every Thanksgiving,
　　He's been drunk, and he's acted so bad.

" Though I work like a nailor till midnight,
　　He'd spend the last cent of his wages ;
Even what I've been raisin' and scrapin'
　　He's thrown to the dogs in his rages.

" As he started this morning for market,
　　I begged him to keep from the cup ;
And I sent Jack along to coax him
　　From the rum-shops, and hurry him up.

" O if only this once he'd come sober,
　　I'm sure that our home would be blest :
Then he and myself and the children
　　Could offer up thanks like the rest.

" But hark !　He's out at the gateway !
　　Run Mabel, and open the door !"
Jack alone stepped over the threshold ;
　　Jack alone stood there on the floor.

He was only a lad of twelve summers,
　　But the flash in his tearful eye
And the flush on his cheek were tell-tales
　　Of a wounded pride yet high.

" I won't go again with Papa !"
　　He said, " for everyone
Says, when they see us passing,
　　' There's the drunkard and his son !'

" Just as we went by Johnson's,
　　The servant called out, ' Net and Floy,
Come in here, my dears, from the side-walk,
　　There's the drunkard and his boy !'

" Yes, Mamma, they never know me
　　As Jack, but, ' The drunkard's son !'"
Here he faltered : his tears fell faster ;
　　He retired to a corner alone.

Away turned his mother in silence,
    Her heart was too full to speak,
And something bright, like a teardrop,
    Rolled down her careworn cheek.

Hark ! another step at the gateway !
    And Mabel flings open the door ;
Her father stept over the threshold—
    Her father stood there on the floor.

He smiled, though his face was haggard
    And his eyes with a newer light shone,
But he moaned as he glanced at the corner
    Where Jack sat weeping alone.

Then he went, with a step unsteady,
    As one that's influenced by wine,
And kissed Jack, and whispered hoarsely,
    "Come now, my dear boy, and don't whine !

"I don't blame you, Jack, but your blushes
For me will arise no more,
    For I've just came straight from the chapel,
Where an abstenance lasting I swore.

"Yes, I swore, and I mean to stick by it,
    No matter what else may be done,
And no one can say when they see us :
    'There's the drunkard and his son !'"

The mother then called them to dinner,
    And voices rose merry and gay ;
And a heartfelt thanksgiving was offered ;
    No souls were more earnest than they.

The turkey and pie seemed more tempting,
    And the pudding more richness displayed,
And the children, O how they attacked them !
    And O what havoc they made.

But suffice it to say, that the father
    Never afterwards dampened their joy ;
For these words always echoed within him,
    "The drunkard and his boy."

A PRAYING AND TRUSTING.

Our minister once was heard to say,
   "Were I humble and poor I'd be blest;
So, for humbleness to my great Father I'll pray,
   And I'll trust to my church for the rest."

MORNING HYMN.

To prayer, to prayer! The blushes of morn
Are deepening fast— the day-spring is born—
   While Heaven's vast eye in its radiance laughs,
   And Nature from life's holy fountain quaffs.
Come, pour to the skies, to our God, a glad prayer!
May its echoes take birth and forever live there.

To prayer! the day and its cares are awake,
And yesterday ne'er from her slumber shall break!
   Her morrow is here; 'tis another to-day;
   Act, act for the best ere it passes away.
With God and with duty enthroned in the breast
O how could the wide world make mortal more blest?

EVENING HYMN.

To prayer, to prayer! Day loses her smile,
And twilight's dim frown waxes deeper the while;
   And night will soon wing o'er the azure deep,
   And hush our cares into halcyon sleep.
O Father of Mercy, thy marvels I see!
My trust is in Thee! My trust is in Thee!

To prayer! for fled is the day's hierarch,
And ornate with new splendor is Heaven's wide arc;
   The moon and the star and the meteoroid
   Emparadise earth from the crystal void;
O Author of Wonders! great Father of Light,
Vouchsafe but to smile on my soul through the night.

OUR DUTY.

O disconsolate man, why fret and complain
That no use was thy birth, that thy life hath been vain?
Bear in mind, every mortal that ever draws breath
Has a duty assigned to fulfill before death;
And thou hast thine own, be it great, be it small,
And perhaps unaware thou art true to it all.
Hast thou e'er helped a bosom to banish distress?
Hast thou e'er helped a heart into happiness?

Hast thou played with the children, and taught them to
    play?
Hast thou prayed with the children, and taught them to
    pray?
Hast thou smiled on the good? hast thou frowned upon
    sin?
Hast thy heart felt the glow of true kindness within?
Ay, thy duty is such; yet it may be well done
By a tear and kind word for the desolate one;
Yea, e'en but one sigh for a mortal in pain
Were enough to convince that thy life is not vain.

THE HAUNTED FOREST.

I had a dream of woe and weal
    That wrought a spell on me,
Which to remember makes me feel
    Its nameless ecstacy.

Methought the pale moon's pensive rays
    Came floating through the wood,
Red'ning the evening's purple haze,
    And wrapped me in their flood.

Upon my burning brow they smiled,
    My burning cheek they kissed;
My fever that had reigned so wild
    No longer could exist.

I wandered 'neath wide-spreading oaks,
   That stood like giants grand,
Arrayed in leafy summer cloaks,
   Woven by Nature's hand.

Two wavy willows soon I spied,
   Soft swaying to and fro,
With drooping branches, green and wide,
   That swept the grass below.

Their plumed trunks rose proud and tall,
   Their boughs did interlace,
Forming a canopy and wall,
   An arcade blent with grace.

A lovelier spot has never been,
   Save Eden in her bloom :
Rare flowers and foliage smiled serene,
   Scatt'ring their sweet perfume.

It seemed, the fay, Enchantment, shook
   Her wand of love and balm,
Sending her magic o'er the brook,
   And wind and wave were calm.

The charm which hung about the place
   Gave nameless thrills that bless
The soul—O who would not embrace
   Such taintless happiness !

Here, 'neath the archway, so ornate,
   A lifeless oak I found :
Blasted it lay ; some early fate
   Had dashed it to the ground.

'Twas mangled limb from limb away ;
   It formed a broken span ;
There in destruction did it lay,
   Like many a fallen man.

"Ah, well aday!" methought it sighed,—
  "Alas for me! alas!
In youth did ruin me betide
  To grovel on the grass!

"Time was when I stood just as straight
  As thou art standing now,
Till frowned a tempest in its hate,
  And rent me bough from bough.

"Here an unhallowed thing I lie,
  Death e'er assailing me :
Ay, always dying, yet cannot die,
  Through all eternity.

"While time's ydrad, envenomed fangs
  Gnaw at my corse unhearsed,
And slow decay yeans deathless pangs :
  Each yeanling is accursed.

"Ah, lackaday! ah, lackaday!
  That life had e'er been tasted!
Youth is all hope and smiles to-day ;
  To-morrow, it is blasted!

"Gramercy! what a sin-bound snare
  Environs the heart's estate!
I conjure thee, O man, beware!
  Take heed ere thou art late!"

Struck dumb to hear that mystic sound
  Take voice within the tree,
I glanced with ill forebodings round,
  But no live thing could see.

'Twas strange, indeed, most wondrous strange,
  To hear a tree deplore,
And then to words of warning change :
  I marveled more and more.

And down I sat, out-wrought, dim-brained,
  By leaden thoughts oppressed ;
And, though my courage still remained,
  Somehow I could not rest.

I strove to reason, but in vain,
  My thoughts, like vapor, flew ;
Nor could I banish from my brain
  That voice which ghastlier grew.

Louder and louder with despair
  Still rang the words of fate,—
" I conjure thee, O man, beware !
  Take heed ere thou art late !"

The cold sweat soon impearled my brow,
  My hands were heavy as lead,
My breath came gasping long and slow,
  And my heart grew chilled and dead.

With one convulsive throb I laughed,—
  " Ha ! ha ! away, ye dreams !
Mine is a sick mind that has quaffed
  Fever's fantastic themes !"

My wild voice echoed more than thrice,
  And ghost-like fluttered round ;
And in a trice I felt like ice,
  And stiffened in a swound.

While cold, imprisoned in that trance,
  My soul within awoke,
And winds and plants gave utterance,
  And bird and brooklet spoke.

PROMETHEUS BOUND.

A MONODY.

PROMETHEUS BOUND.

A MONODY.

Here on this crag, this solitary peak,
Where yawn abysses, bottomless and bleak,
Whose sunless grots give forth no voice of life,
Am I fast bound, beyond all hope of strife,
Chained by the hand of Vulcan,—woe is me!
What god will dare to cancel Jove's decree?

Here am I doomed to wither on the rocks,
Before the gaze of mortals, and of flocks
That throng the free realm of the feathered race,
Whilst fair condoling nymphs with words of grace
But rend my wounds the wider.   All is vain!
Ay, naught created can assuage my pain!

The cloud-compellor has decreed my fate,
That I for time unlimited must wait
The hour when once again I shall have risen,
Unfettered from this grief-infested prison.
Yet that alone were gambol to endure,
Could I from deadlier ills remain secure.

'Tis not that I writhe, blasted and o'erthrown,
Nor the contortions of my limbs I moan;
'Tis not this iron bolt through my quivering frame,
The links and rivets forged in Vulcan's flame,
For even the vulture, glutting full his maw,
Tearing my liver with his gory claw,
My steaming liver, which grows on the while,
To cloy that monster with new flesh and bile.
Not even these is it that wrings my heart,
But O, ye furies, how shall I impart

The coming baleful burdens, mountain-high !
Yet live I must, a Titan cannot die !
O woes on woes, unnumbered, still before me !
'Tis they that whelm the pangs relentless o'er me.

Not immortality alone doth curse,
But power to know the future ; that is worse,
Far worse than all the ills I undergo ;
That is the fuel to my scorching woe.

Yet this, all this, tho' now beyond control,
Were not so dire, so baneful to my soul,
Had I but merited e'en half the fate
Decreed to me by Jove's unbridled hate ;
But oh ! for generous deeds I grovel, trod,
Crushed by the malice of a self-willed god,
Flouted by all gods in my woe-girt plight ;
And why ? Ask why ! O for some starless night,
Some rayless blackness to obscure entire
The emblazoned heart, the eye's indignant fire,
The impious smile of ridicule and scorn
That needs must e'en by mortals all be worn,
When that ephemeral race shall hear me tell
The sin for which I suffer such a hell.

'Twas this, forsooth : My tender heart gave way
In pity to those creatures of a day,
Who, compassed 'round with ills innumerable,
Dragged on their life, a transitory spell—
Its fleetness being their solitary boon.
What eye could such despairs not importune
To gracious tears ? What ear could they not gain ?
What heart, though adamant, could they not pain ?

Mine did they wrench ; they smote upon mine ears ;
I wept—yea, wept ; the vapory clouds of tears
Bedewed my tremulous features ; then did I,
Alone of all the immortal deity,

Descend with gifts to that ill-fated race.
My high prerogatives with liberal grace
I lavished on them. First, I gave them fire,
The kindliest boon a mortal could desire.

And O, to see the change, the wondrous change !
New beings all, mankind's whole world grew strange.
No more could human forms be seen adrift,
Hither and thither tossed by Heaven's whims,
Without self motion in their frozen limbs—
Their nerves benumbed with bitter wind and frost :
No more in midnight's blackness were they lost,
Compelled on hand and knee to creep abroad,
By touch and instinct seeking out the road :
But everywhere was found a happiness—
The blazing hearth, which mortal aye shall bless,
Girt round by faces radiant with cheer,
Fond parents, children, gods that they revere,
And lamplight shed a lustre o'er the room,
And made what was till then unknown, a home :
And moonless midnight mocked the smile of day
With torch to light the traveler on his way.

Nor was this all ; with personal command,
I taught how dwellings 'neath the human hand
Could rear themselves into a stately form,
A shield impregnable to sun and storm,
Free from the insects and the bats and owls,
Which haunt their former 'bodes, within the bowels
Of cavernous mountains and of rock-flank'd hills,
But dare not follow with their odious ills.

On man, moreover, were bestowed by me
Blind hopes, that he the future might not see ;
Else ne'er could he have smiled. 'Twas, next to fire,
The kindliest boon a mortal could desire.

Then snow-winged chariots of the sea I gave
To buffet the inhospitable wave,

And, at my word, o'er highway and o'er plain,
Refulgent cars were seen to whirl amain,
Whose brazen ribs and highly-burnished seats
Flashed scintillating brilliance, such as beats
A blindness into many a staring eye,
And draws down envy from the etherial sky ;
And all the gods waxed rancorous at me
To see man cinctured with such fulgency.

Nor did I cease to give : art followed art,
Science on science gushed into the heart
And blazed a bright, bright reason in the breast,
Which made man like a god, a being blest—
A reason bright, next to blind hopes and fire,
The kindliest boon a mortal could desire.

All these into that race did I instill,
Then fell 'neath Jove's inexorable will,
A lesson to long ages yet to come !
I see the future and it makes my doom
The heavier ; a similar fate shall bind
All benefactors of enthralled mankind.
O right has turned to wrong, and wrong to right !
And justice has deserted day and night !

The thundering sun of Saturn craves no good,
But evil, evil, evil is his food ;
E'en for such crimes as he himself commits
He showers down vengeance in fierce thunder-fits
Upon mankind ; his vengeful bolts are hurled
From erring world below to erring world,
In hideous guise, as punishment divine,
And smite transgressor lewd and libertine,
While he himself back to his couch retires,
Where Venus flames lascivious desires,
Where vile, incestuous nuptials give delight,
And nymphs succumb, responsive to his might.

And lecherous goddesses his wish obey,
Whose brazen fronts offend the god of day.
Out, out upon him! I blaspheme and curse
That all-corruptor of the universe!

Not wondrous were it to behold all heaven
Into a thousand wide-jawed chasms riven,
Flecked with the fiery paths of meteors;
To see old ocean overleap his shores,
Great rivers retrograde, rush toward their source,
The moon stand doubtful midway in her course,
Eastward the chariot of the sun career,
And every star shoot headlong from its sphere.
Not these were marvels now, not e'en the worst!
Since virtue's dead and justice is reversed.

Yet thou, Oceanus, the staunchest friend
Prometheus knows, thou blindly wouldst ascend
To that all-miscreative tyrant, Jove,
Before the taunts of every god above,
With prayer and importunity for grace
From one that has no grace, but malice base—
All-withering malice, rage and dastard hate,
Which no submission can propitiate—
Submission? I submit? and to his rod?
He is my slave, my menial, not my god!

Yea, heed me! in response to thy request,
The unhallowed king, the omnipotent unblest,
Forgetful of all ancient favors tasted,
Will hurl thee to perdition, ever blasted,
Impaled in lightless flames, invested round
With Stygian agonies without a bound.

No, my Oceanus, O go not there!
No prayer for me, nor thought, nor sign of prayer
Shall ever seek a being that I scorn,
Whose craven face insults the light of morn,

Who, loveless, faithless, sways the imperial rod,
Of gods the most unfit to be a god—
A spirit I despise, detest, abhor,
And shall despise, and shall for evermore,
A deathless adversary ; hate and curse !
My direst imprecations, ay, worse, worse !
Threats unrevealed shall storm his foul, foul heart,
Each threat a pang, a woe-envenomed dart.

Nor will I fear, nor need I fear ; I'm 'reft
Well nigh of sense—small pain, small solace left ;
So let him lord it even as he list,
Invent new hell-racks to disjoint and twist ;
Annihilate he can not, god of the sky,
For live I must, a Titan can not die.
Yet death were sweet, since free from agony,
But such were triumph to my foe o'er me,
And smells of vanquishment. No, furies, no !
Lacerate, tear with sharp-fanged woe on woe !
Woe is my element, as wrong is his,
As jealousy, as guilt, as hatred is ;
As hate shall e'en be mine, time yet to be,
When down shall crash his tottering dynasty.

Then will great Jove his ancient friends recall,
The warrior gods that wrought his father's fall,
And him instated on the heavenly throne,
And gave a wisdom to be his alone ;
Sons of Uranus and of Earth were they,
The race of mighty Titans ; yet the pay
For this old friendship, this high service given,
Ten thousand black reproaches flings to heaven.
I, in return for favors done of old,
Am chained and crucified for years untold.

Atlas, my brother, strong and terrible,
Dreaded alike by Saturn and deep hell,

Groans 'neath the incommensurable weight
Of heaven's star-burdened vault, a pillar great.
Mighty, yet vacillating 'neath the strain
Of worlds on worlds his shoulders e'er sustain,
Seeming eternally about to fall ;
Yet does not fall, for Jove's accursed thrall
Fates him to stand in endless, vast endeavor,
Half tipping o'er forever, ever, ever !

And his own tresses, miles long, disentwined,
Hither and thither ride the furious wind,
And lash his limbs with venomous blow on blow,
While from a million wide-mouthed wounds there flow
Streams of dark crimson, which his barren tears
Swell to a turbulent tide, and no one hears
His lamentation, for his bitterness
He moans and wails in murmurs echoless.

Alas ! his irremediable plight !
His breast in sharp-tooth'd, vaporous flames is dight,
Which gnaw its inmost core and spit despair,
An ineradicable venom, there.

Thus bound and damned forever does he sigh ;
Still, live he must, a Titan cannot die.
He, in return for favors done of old,
Is chained and blasted there for years untold.

Typhon, my earth-born brother, hundred-headed,
Whose prowess furies, hell and Saturn dreaded,
Writhes, disempowered and whelmed and bound, beneath
Etna's stupendous mountain, while his breath,
All sulphurous, flaming, lurid, bursts her crest ;
And he, stretched prone in bitterest unrest
And anguish—anguish, O ineffable !
Encinctured 'round by fires that hiss and yell,
He rolls and turns, in vain he turns and rolls,
Upheaving from the mount's infernal bowels

Lava and boulders, which are headlong hurled,
A havoc wide into the outer world;
And burnt is he, e'en to a cinder burnt,
His hundred heads to a hundred crisps are turnt.
Thus evermore he moans in agony;
Still, live he must, a Titan can not die.
He in return for favors done of old,
Is chained and blasted there for years untold.

Ingratitude! ingratitude! what name
Enough misshapen for thy monstrous frame!
But words are idle: there will come a time
When Heaven shall vomit forth her vice and crime,
Nor shadows shall there be of things that are.
O Ion, hapless maiden, driven afar,
From land to land, o'er sea, o'er forest dun,
O'er snow-capp'd mounts that neighbor on the sun—
Thou, whom enamored Jupiter gives chase,
For ever thwarted—thou, whose beauteous face,
Sought by the love, then by the fierce displeasure
Of highest God, grieves thee beyond all measure—
Do thou take heart! thou art a glorious maid;
Full thrice three thousand-fold shalt thou be paid
For all thy woe, thy blood-traced aberrations.
Glory is thine: with ten more generations,
The third of thine own lineage, dire to see,
Shall overthrow Jove's hated dynasty.

Then Jove shall fall e'en as his sire of yore;
Jove, evil's microcosm, shall reign no more.
Then, then that king will envy me my doom;
His shade, diminished to a ghost of gloom,
Shall sink forever through the boundless void,
Inflamed in ether like a meteoroid—
Down, down his course, forever downward thrown—
Down through the dark abysm—down—ever down.

But ho ! a gale ! the sea begins to fry !
Daughter of Imachus, take warning, fly !
The deep-toned billow from its slumber breaks ;
The limitless expanse of ether quakes ;
Now all the elements are impelled to motion :
Embroiled is black-browed Heaven with the ocean,
And there and there portentous fire appears—
See, see ! he nears—Jove's gaunt phantasm nears,
And nears his chained, though still unvanquished, foe
To poison more my unrepented woe.

Flee, flee, ye nymphs ! ye children of the sea—
Ye daughters of prolific Thetis—flee,
Lest share ye my unenviable fate—
Flee, mother, flee ! escape the avenger's hate !

The thunderbolts dart, three-fold interwoven ;
Vales sever, adamantine rocks are cloven—
Woe, woe is me ! the fell inventions new !
Anguish ! eternal anguish ! *Eleleu !*
Ah, *Eleleu !* ah me ! my lidless eyes !
Pangs rend my heart, as lightnings rend the skies—
Pain ! inextinguishable pain ! Yet I,
Imperishable, can not, would not die !
Still no submission ! No ! forever no !
Food of my soul, unutterable woe !
Agony, fire-fanged agony and lasting !
No sleep, no rest, but endless pain and blasting !
Pain, pain envenomed, never ceasing, never !
Pain, pain, all pain, forever, ever, ever.